THE MAGIC LAUNDRY:

STORIES

By

Jacob M. Appel

Snake~Nation~Press
Valdosta, Georgia

Snake Nation Press wishes to thank:
Barbara Passmore & The Price-Campbell Foundation
The Georgia Council for the Arts
Gloria & Wilby Coleman
Lowndes/Valdosta Arts Commission
Dean Poling & *The Valdosta Daily Times*
Blake Ellis
Our Subscribers

Snake Nation Press, the only independent literary press in south Georgia, publishes two *Snake Nation Reviews,* a book of poetry by a single author each year, and a book of fiction by a single author each year. Unsolicited submissions of fiction, essays, art, and poetry are welcome throughout the year but will not be returned unless a stamped, self-addressed envelope is included. We encourage simultaneous submissions.

Subscriptions
Individuals $30
Institutions $40
Foreign $40
Sample Copy $12 (includes shipping)

Published by Snake Nation Press
110 West Force Street
Valdosta, Georgia 31601

Printed and bound in the United States of America.

ISBN: 978-0-9883029-9-0

THE MAGIC LAUNDRY:
STORIES

by
Jacob M. Appel

Snake Nation Press is a small non-profit press
dedicated to publishing literature
in all its myriad forms.
110 Force Street
Valdosta, GA 31601
www.snakenationpress.org

Acknowledgements

"The Magic Laundry" in *Columbia Journal*
"Enoch Arden's One Night Stands" in *Beloit Fiction Journal*
"The Ataturk of the Outer Boroughs" in *Raritan*
"Natural Selection" in *Gulf Stream*
"Exposure" in *Sycamore Review*
"The House Call" in *Shenandoah*
"The Empress of Charcoal" in *Harpur Palate*
"Animal Control" in *Potomac Review*

Table of Contents

DEDICATION

For my parents, who have to put up with me, and for Rosalie, who chooses to do so.

Natural Selection

The stolen baboon. On the evening news, she's an irrelevancy—a simian mug shot tucked between National Hairball Awareness Day and an interview with the Boston Strangler's children. Six hours later, she's lounging on the sofa in our living room, smacking together her protruded lips, scratching her back on the damask. Suburban Tampa is apparently far more fun than a lab cage in Atlanta. At Emory, they didn't have a baby-grand piano to pound with her toes. Or curtains to swing from until the rods collapse. Or a cornucopia of plastic fruit. Pears. Bananas. Pineapple. She pelts these at me, one after another. When the fruit bowl runs dry, she lobs coffee table books, a bouquet of irises crafted from Matsuno beads. Her deep-set eyes look curious and playful; her rhythmic grunting sounds friendly, even gentle. But I am in no mood for games. The occasion calls for composure. Damage Control. Later, after Mrs. Bonzo has been returned to sender, there will be time to wring my daughter's neck.

"This is just unacceptable," I say. "You've crossed a line."

Tabitha sits with her chin braced on the back of a dining room chair. She is munching on sunflower seeds. Her eyes wander impatiently. I imagine she acts no differently from any other college sophomore, home for spring break, being chewed out by a beleaguered father. Her look is new since Christmas: a torn T-shirt, too large, screen-printed with an iconic Che Guevara. Rope sandals. Matted auburn hair. It strikes me that there is a slight sag to her breasts, a definition to her nipples—my daughter has abandoned her brassiere. All that is fine, of course. I'm a child of the sixties. I've described my own father, a professor of jurisprudence, as "well-intentioned" and "hopelessly bourgeois." If anybody can sympathize with a bit of youthful idealism, it should be me. But this is different. This is a federal crime. According to the legal commentator on channel seven, this may qualify as terrorism.

"Good God, Tabby," I say. "What were you thinking?"

"Do you know what they were going to do to her?" demands Tabitha. "They were going to cut her spinal cord. Intentionally. On the off chance they might be able to reattach it later."

"So you had to steal her?"

"Liberate her," retorts Tabitha. "How would you feel if somebody paralyzed you for their own amusement?"

I recognize the matter is far more complex than this—that the research at Emory, whatever its drawbacks, is not being conducted whimsically. They say the experiments may help quadriplegics walk again. I'm a conservation biologist. I have no way of knowing whether they are correct. Nor is this a matter I want to get into while a stolen baboon is beating the stuffing from my pillows.

"So you *appropriated* her," I say, neutrally. "You had to bring her home?"

"Her name's Kidogo. It means 'little one' in Swahili."

The baboon, as though on cue, sweeps across the coffee table and topples the stand of fire pokers. She appears to be grinning.

I ignore the mounting damage as best I can. I feel like the musicians performing with equanimity as the *Titanic* goes under.

"Couldn't one of your friends take her home?" I ask, desperately.

"They took the rabbits and the rats."

"Of course," I say. "The rabbits and the rats."

"It was a big operation," explains Tabitha. "We had only one chance."

A big operation—I picture them sporting ski masks, secretly stockpiling rabbit feed and carambolas. "The Great Train Robbery" meets *Watership Down.*

I'm not sure how to respond to all this. Tabitha has always been a good girl, studious, top of her class. Pretty, too, like her mother was. Large eyes. Delicate chin. The truth is—at some point even a widowed father of an only daughter must admit this—boys like her. They want her. Enough to send roses, unsolicited letters. They throw pebbles at her bedroom window, beg short strolls to bare their hearts. I suspect some are luckier than others. That's her business. I've never asked. But then something like this happens, a case study in calamitous judgment, and you question how you've been so lax. At fifty-eight, I find it hard to understand why a popular, apolitical girl suddenly risks her future for the welfare of a gelada baboon.

"I could lose my job for this," I say. "We could go to jail."

Kidogo finds this amusing. She yanks a photograph from the wall, one of the prints I shot while rafting the Amazon. The picture sails over our heads. Its glass frame shatters against the mahogany sideboard.

Tabitha is now sobbing. She's driven straight through the night—she must be exhausted to the bone. Her bags are still in the Plymouth.

"I'm sorry, Dad," she says. "You don't understand. I had to."

"I know," I say, soothingly. "I'm sure you did."

Not certain is why Charles Robert Darwin, my relative and namesake, started scribbling the journal entries that would become *The Origin of Species*. I was pondering this very question—a matter central to my manuscript—when Tabitha, who happens to be his great-great-grand niece, arrived with the baboon.

A bit about my book: It will be entitled *Darwin on Darwin*. It is part of a series. They've already put out Clement Freud on his grandfather, and the anthropologist Selma Einstein-Loewenthal on her cousin, Albert. The volume wasn't my idea. I am writing at the urging of Francine Garvey, who teaches with me in the department of biology. Francine is the planet's foremost authority on ivory-billed woodpeckers. She searches for them, every spring, in Cuba's Sierra Maestra. There is a strong possibility that the birds—last sighted in 1987—have gone extinct. There is also a possibility that Francine is Tabitha's future stepmother. *This last part,* Tabitha doesn't know. Nor, though she carries his genes, has "Uncle Charlie" ever drawn my daughter's interest.

Back to Darwin. One theory contends that he suffered, after the age of thirty-five, from a panic disorder. The naturalist experienced "uncomfortable palpitations of the heart," also a fear he was "going mad." He shunned social engagements—preferring, instead, to read Thomas Malthus and to correspond with authorities on animal husbandry. The recent Cambridge graduate who boarded the *HMS Beagle* in 1831 was a gregarious dandy distinguished by his passion for hunting, shooting and cards. By 1845, he was somber and reclusive. According to psychiatric authorities, an acute shock or stress often precedes the onset of such chronic, debilitating anxiety. A chief suspect in this case: The death of Darwin's daughter, Mary Eleanor.

Tabitha falls asleep in the living room and I carry her upstairs. It's been at least a decade since I cradled my daughter's body like this, a life time since I tucked the flannel blanket around her delicate shoulders. Her heft surprises me. She's added pounds since grade school, a "freshman fifteen" on top of her "adolescent fifty." Sleeping, she seems to weigh extra—like a lifeless kitten. I adjust the pillows under her head, drawing the knotted bangs from her eyes. I kiss her on the forehead. Downstairs, I hear Kidogo barking sharply. I can also hear the television: an inopportune rerun, the late Marlin Perkins introducing *Mutual of Omaha's Wild Kingdom.* Our baboon is no lucky monkey. She's tuned to "Leopards of the Serengeti." Now she's terrified, flipping her black lips, emitting high-pitched wails. Serves her right, I think.

My next step is baboon-proofing the house. For this, there's no twelve-step program, no *Primate Management for Dummies.* You have to learn on the job, build sequentially like Robinson Crusoe or Swiss Family Robinson. It's part science, part art—for both of us. We discover she's too heavy to use the chandeliers as vines, gifted at finger-painting with feces. Initially, I'd kept her off the enclosed terrace, afraid her clamor might draw attention from the neighbors. That was a mistake, I see now. Keeping her in the living room, even overnight, is impossible. Kidogo's temporary home will have to be the side porch, though this means replacing the screens with storm windows. The job takes two hours—including twenty minutes icing the thumb I've crushed in the stepladder. Around dawn, I nail a heavy chenille bedspread over the glass. This will keep Kidogo hidden from view. (Unfortunately, it will also keep out the light—everything except for a glimmer of day at the edges of the cloth. There's no choice. I cannot risk Kidogo alone with electric cords, lightbulbs.) It takes nearly another hour, and a dozen frozen grapes, to lure the baboon onto the darkened veranda.

When I wake up around noon, Tabitha is already gone. She's left a plate of toast crusts and a quarter glass of milk on the kitchen table. She's also left a note:

GONE TO LUNCH AND A MOVIE.
PLEASE TAKE CARE OF KIDOGO.
LUV U. TAB
PS: CAN YOU GET HER CUCUMBERS & GRASSHOPPERS?

The baboon, mercifully, is still asleep. She's managed to topple the vintage telephone cabinet we inherited from my mother-in-law, and she's cuddled against its side, her head propped on an aquamarine vinyl hatbox. I tiptoe back into the kitchen, sliding shut the porch door behind me. Still in my bathrobe and slippers, I retrieve the morning paper from the front yard. It's cool for April. There's a breeze blowing off the Gulf. The frangipani have unfurled their tricolors, dancing over an ocean of white gardenias. This should be an afternoon spent in the flower beds, transplanting day lilies, pruning tea roses. Unfortunately, the lead headline in *Tribune* reads, FBI: NO MONKEY BUSINESS IN LAB HEIST. Kidogo is also the top story on public radio, the midday TV news. A combination of national politics and human interest. Fortified, of course, by images of cuddly animals. The Berkeley-based "Animals First" has claimed responsibility. They've offered to barter Kidogo for a testing moratorium. The Attorney General has derided the perpetrators as "a fifth column of the Eco-Taliban."

Kidogo raps on the porch door. When I draw open the glass, she vaults from the folding table onto my shoulder; another jump lands her atop the refrigerator. She inspects me closely as I go about my business. We are out of instant coffee. Also cucumbers, grasshoppers. "You'll have to settle for bananas and water," I say. Kidogo pokes her nose forward and clutches the air with her hands. I suddenly feel guilty, as though I'm running a primate penitentiary. "Okay, okay," I say. "I'll go get you something. But you're going to wait on the porch." It's not that easy, of course. I don't want to draw suspicion, so I can't buy too many supplies at one location. By the time I return—my Saturn loaded with unbreakable mirrors, miniature tires, commercial primate food—Tabitha's Plymouth is already parked in the driveway.

My daughter's crouched on the porch, slapping around a ball with the baboon. It's a lightweight, rainbow beachball. She's dressed Kidogo in one of my cotton T-shirts. The shirt has DARWIN FAMILY REUNION emblazoned across the chest. I imagine my daughter finds this amusing.

"You had no business going out like that," I say.

"What was I supposed to do? It was the first day of spring break. Don't you think my friends would have gotten suspicious?"

I hadn't thought of it this way. "That's not the point."

Tabitha claps the baboons hands together several times; afterwards, Kidogo repeats the clapping gesture unassisted. "She's very smart," says Tabitha.

"We can't go on like this," I warn her. "This is an untenable situation."

Tabitha looks up, pleading. "We'll keep her hidden. Nobody will know."

"Sweet Jesus, Tabby. She's practically destroyed the house. How am I supposed to invite people over?"

"You don't have people over anyway," she says.

"I do, sometimes," I insist. "Hasn't it even crossed your mind that I might be dating again? That I might have a girlfriend?"

Tabitha hugs the beachball to her chest. "No," she answers. "It hasn't." This isn't an objection, I understand—simply an observation. And the truth is that I'm not dating, that I haven't dated in the eight years since Annie drowned. Francine Garvey isn't a girlfriend. She's merely a prospect.

"There's a nationwide monkey hunt going on, Tabby. Do you understand how serious this is? You have to take her back."

"I *do* understand how serious this is," she answers.

Kidogo raises herself on her hind legs, sniffing. Tabitha tosses her a piece of sliced mango.

"Maybe we could leave her somewhere," I suggest. "After all this attention, they won't dare hurt her."

"You don't know the first thing about baboons, do you?" retorts Tabitha. She says this as though it's the most degrading putdown. "She'll find her way back."

"To Atlanta?"

"To here, Dad. Baboons have homing instincts, sort of like pigeons. Anywhere you take her, she'll lead the F.B.I. right to your door."

"You've got to be kidding," I say. "We can't be stuck with her forever."

I frown at the baboon. She responds by squeezing the mango slice in her fist, letting the juice ooze between her fingers. Then—without warning—she jumps into my arms. Her nose is only inches from mine. She apparently wants to rub them together. Her long fingers grab at my face, leaving a fruity thumbprint on my glasses. I am suddenly nervous, overwhelmed. I recognize this feeling. I've known it before. It is being the parent of a young child. Against my better judgment, I rock Kidogo in my arms.

14

"What do you know about an organization called Animals First?" I ask Tabitha.

She shrugs. "Never heard of them."

"I didn't think so," I say.

I keep rocking. The baboon gurgles like a baby.

My great-granduncle's forty-three year marriage to his first cousin, Emma Wedgwood, was repeatedly marred by tragedy. Only seven of their ten children survived to adulthood. Mary Eleanor, as I've mentioned, died of diphtheria in 1842. Her death coincided with her father's retreat from Victorian society. During the next seven years, the naturalist expanded his trove of display beetles, at its time the most impressive entomological collection in Europe, and penned an obscure treatise about barnacles. His ideas on natural selection remained private. They were heretical, after all. Unlawful. Moreover, Darwin was a communicant of the Church of England. He'd studied theology at Christ's Church. A publicity-shy ex-divinity student, particularly one dependant on a government fellowship, wasn't a good candidate to radicalize "the species problem." But then his daughter, ten year old Anne Elizabeth, succumbed to tuberculosis. Annie's death drove her father to atheism. His notes on natural selection rapidly became the most widely kept secret in England.

Darwin argued for gradual evolution. In recent years, a competing school of thought led by the late Harvard geologist Stephen Jay Gould has championed 'punctuated equilibrium'—the theory that change occurs in sudden bursts. That has certainly been the case for me. Tabitha's birth catapulted me into adulthood. My own Annie's death—dragged off by a riptide at forty-seven—reordered my priorities. Ballet recitals and trick-or-treating rose in the pecking order; botany expeditions fell off the map. And now a third transformation. Kidogo. I watch her playing dress-up with Tabitha. They are working through my daughter's childhood wardrobe. This afternoon, the baboon's decked out in a blue dress with anchors embroidered on the shoulders. A red neck bandanna. A sailor's cap. She looks a bit like Ethel Merman in *Anything Goes*. Tabitha holds the mirror for her, letting her poke at her reflection with long, pointy fingers. I haven't seen my daughter so happy since Annie's death. I've been watching her all week. I've accomplished nothing on my manuscript. I haven't even returned Francine's phone calls. Six days ago, my future looked as clear as the horizon: writing, gardening, excursions on the Gulf in Francine's speedboat. Now, who knows? I try not to think about what we'll do with the baboon when Tabitha returns to school.

In one way, Darwin had it right. I'd die for Tabitha. I'd kill for Tabitha. It's impossible for me to understand surviving the loss of a child. Maybe that is why writing about my great-granduncle brings me to tears. He did not attend the reading of his seminal paper, *The Origin of Species*, at the Linnean Society on July 1, 1858. His favorite son, Charles Waring, had died of scarlet fever three days before.

I read the headlines on the Sunday *Tribune* with relief. Every morning we've been the lead story: NO LIGHT ON MONKEYSHINES; ALL POINTS BANANAS IN BABOON HUNT. Fortunately, there's been an apocalyptic earthquake in Peru over the weekend, and the governor of Florida's confessed to cross-dressing, so we're out of the paper. That's how it works on the Gulf Coast. Either you're page one, or you're yesterday's news. The rest is all sports, obits, crime blotter. That's usually frustrating. Today, it's a gift from the gods. I shuffle back into the house, feeling as though I've knocked the scythe from death's arms. "You may be home free yet, you dumb baboon," I announce. "Papayas on the house! What do you say to that?"

Tabitha stumbles down the stairs, rubbing her eyes. It is early afternoon. Caring for a two-year-old baboon has addled our sleep cycles. "What's going on?"

I hand her the newspaper. "Our fifteen minutes of fame are over," I say. I've already done a calculus in my head: It took them eighteen years to catch the Unabomber, twenty-one to nab the Jackal. The Zodiac Killer is still on the lamb. Comparatively, we're small potatoes. To celebrate, I peel the skin off a cucumber. That's when I'm struck by the silence from the porch. No pounding. No wailing. Not so much as one guttural moan. I slide open the screen door, still carrying the cucumber.

"Kidogo!" I shout. "What the hell——?"

She's gone, of course. The hatbox stands atop the ironing board, an improvised stepstool, and the bedspread has been torn from its perch. During the night, Kidogo has managed to unscrew one of the storm windows. They don't call baboons "mimic monkeys" for nothing. All those hours watching me work with the phillips head, she was bound to pick up the

16

basics of carpentry. Outside, a soft breeze flutters the magnolias. A pair of purple gallinules cavort beside the canal. In the distance loom the shore-front highrises, hostile concrete watchtowers. Tracking a baboon around Tampa Bay would be both foolhardy and futile.

I sit down at the kitchen table, unnerved. Tabitha combs the porch, peeking behind lawn chairs and under stacks of plywood. "Maybe she's just hiding," she pleads. "Maybe she's playing a game." Her eyes are glazed, slightly bloodshot. Pillow stuffing hangs in her hair. My daughter looks as though her home has just been blown away by an unexpected hurricane. "Kidogo!" she cries. "Kidogo!"

"Don't. The neighbors will hear."

Tabitha kicks aside two badminton rackets. "Who the hell cares?"

I cross the kitchen and hug my daughter; she practically collapses into my arms. And then the buzzer sounds. Twice. A pause. Three times. I gently push Tabitha back onto her feet. Through the living room curtains, I see two state troopers standing in the portico. One is short with a small nose, protruding ears. His tall, broad companion boasts a chiseled jaw and an overhung brow. They look like toy soldiers plucked off different rungs of the evolutionary ladder. Both men have orange blossoms, the Florida state flower, pinned to their lapels. Uneasily, I inch open the door.

"Good morning, officers," I say. I sense Tabitha behind me in the shadows. My instinct is to obstruct the entryway, to shield her from view.

"Sorry to bother you," says the shorter trooper. He bears a striking resemblance, I realize, to a marmoset. "We're looking for a missing baboon."

What a coincidence, I think. I can feel the blood in my temples.

"We've had several sightings this morning," continued Officer Marmoset. "You haven't seen anything, have you?" He passes me a photograph of the wanted animal—as though to distinguish Kidogo from other baboons afoot in Southwest Florida.

Officer Gorilla looks bored. He tests the strength of the porch swing, pokes at the wasp nest above the drainpipe with a stick.

I shrug at the photo. "I'd remember that face," I say.

Marmoset nods agreeably. "Well if you see anything."

"Of course, of course." We're in the clear. At least for the moment. I flash a plastic smile, gradually inching shut the door. That's when Gorilla takes a sudden wasp sting on the thumb.

"Fuck!" shouts Gorilla. "Fuck! Fuck! Fuck!" The trooper wrings his oversized hand, trying to shake away the pain. As the initial throb recedes, he grins sheepishly. "Sorry about that," he apologizes. "Think I could use your john?"

I have no choice. I direct Gorilla to the downstairs bathroom. Marmoset stands in the foyer, examining the broken chandelier and the overturned hat rack. "You redecorating?" he asks.

"We had a bit of a row," I answer. "All over now."

"I've got the world's worst temper," adds Tabitha.

Marmoset ambles to the cherrywood letter table. He picks up a partially peeled banana and examines it suspiciously. I realize I am still brandishing the vegetable knife and the naked cucumber. The trooper turns to Tabitha. "You in school?" he asks.

She nods.

I'm afraid he'll ask where. Emory is ground zero in the baboon saga. Instead, he says: "Funny time to leave bananas out, isn't it? With a wild monkey on the loose."

It seems he's toying with us. Now's the time, I know, to shout for Tabitha to flee. It's two against one. If I take Marmoset by surprise—tackle him from the side—she might make it. But my daughter's in no condition to escape. She's wearing thin cotton pajamas dappled with miniature teddy bears. These make her look girlish, innocent. Not the outfit I want my daughter displaying for the neighbors. Or even Florida's Finest. That's when I realize Officer Marmoset isn't playing detective. He's flirting with my daughter.

Marmoset grins at his banana remark. "That was a joke," he explains.

"I hope your partner's okay," I say. "I feel dreadful."

I hear Gorilla shut off the bathroom faucet. He returns, his thumb wrapped in toilet tissue. "What's with the primate food?" he asks.

I've realize I've left the feed sack under the sink.

"I'm on a diet," I say. "Anti-Atkins." I pat my stomach for effect.

Gorilla frowns. "Mind if we look around a bit?" he asks.

I try to conceal the knife and cucumber behind my back. "We're actually on our way out," I stammer. "Maybe later."

"Maybe later," echoes Gorilla. "Maybe we'll bring a warrant."

He gives the foyer a once-over as he departs. Marmoset follows, offering Tabitha an apologetic smile. "I guess we'll see you later," he says.

I push shut the door. Nausea is building in my throat. With our narrow escape comes a violent recognition of my own stupidity. How could I possibly hope to conceal a stolen baboon on my veranda? How could I take such risks with Tabitha's future? Kidogo's disappearance—any way you look at it—is a blessing. "Let's clean this place up," I say. "Before they come back."

Tabitha's teeth are chattering. "What's that?" she asks.

There's no mistaking it. A hard knock at the back door. How could I have underestimated Marmoset and Gorilla? Surprise is on their side.

I'm ready to fess up and beg for mercy. I'll plead guilty, if they'll drop the charges against Tabitha. That seems fair. It's unnecessary, of course. Marmoset and Gorilla are not on the back steps. It's Kidogo. Returned. Offering me a hug and a sprig of orange blossoms.

Many philosophers before Darwin had noted the brutality of the natural world, the struggle between the lion and the lamb. What made Darwin's work so original was his focus on conflict within a single species. He wrote about finches competing with finches, relative mating advantages among crabs. Survival of the fittest. The most cynical of all biological theories. A direct contrast to Lamarck's optimistic claim that animals' traits reflect "inner longings" for perfection. One cannot help wondering what set the man's thinking down this pessimistic path.

Two recent biographies emphasize the death of Darwin's mother, Susannah, when the naturalist was only eight. The boy may have developed the seeds of his theory while watching his five siblings, and numerous cousins, compete for the attentions of his widowed father. Interestingly, several studies link genius with the early death of a parent. Newton, Dante and Copernicus all lost parents before the age of seven. This childhood tragedy may also be advantageous from an evolutionary viewpoint. Such a death forces the other parent to be more careful, take fewer risks. I've found that to be the case with me since Annie died. I've quit smoking. I won't go up with Francine in her Cessna. I refuse to collect specimens in the Colombian Cordillera. What choice do I have? Tabitha needs me. The death of a second parent, from the perspective of an individual organism, is an evolutionary calamity.

Our window of opportunity is narrow. The monkey squad may return at any moment, armed with a warrant and a tranquilizer gun. I recognize that the situation demands parenting of the unpopular, bullet-biting sort.

"I've made a decision," I say. Tabitha is cheerful again, bathing Kidogo's soft black fur in the kitchen sink. We've learned the hard way that baboons need regular washing, particularly their rumps and the coarse tufts at the tips of their tails. They cannot be toilet-trained and possess a knack for peeling off diapers. "Please, Tabby. Hear me out."

Tabitha wipes the baboon's nape with a washcloth. "I'm not taking her back," she says, sharply. "I'd rather go to jail."

"Nobody is asking you to take her back," I say. "But she can't stay. You know that. You have to go to school and I have to go back to work. If those cops find her here, it will ruin our lives." My daughter eyes me apprehensively. Kidogo splashes suds onto the countertop.

"I have a colleague," I explain. "She owns a speedboat. She's willing to run the baboon down the coast into Cuba. Or to give it a shot, at least."

"When?"

"Tonight." I'm clenching my fists behind my back, hoping this works. "She'll let her loose on the coast. Near Puerto Esperanza. What do you say?"

"I love her," says Tabitha. "It's not fair."

She's already lost her mother. It tears me apart to watch her go through this again. "I can't see any other way, honey. Trust me."

Tabitha slumps into a kitchen chair, cupping her coffee mug in both palms. She pours chocolate syrup into the coffee. I watch as the syrup oozes glacially from the jar and as my daughter stirs the concoction, then licks off the spoon. "What if I say yes?" she finally asks.

"That's the end of it," I say. "I take her down to the marina and tomorrow morning she wakes up across the water. Baboons can't swim, can they?" Tabitha doesn't smile at this jest, so I add: "Francine knows people in Cuba. I'm sure she'll be looked after. Safer than risking recapture around here."

"I guess," says Tabitha. "Can I come with you to the boat?"

I shake my head. "Best not," I say. "Someone has to straighten this place up before the return of the monkey wardens." I'm not thrilled about leaving Tabitha alone with Officer Marmoset, particularly with Gorilla as chaperone—but the alternative is leaving a trail of coconut shells and citrus rinds that leads straight to Alcatraz. Or Guantanamo. Or wherever they torture monkeynappers. "And Tabby," I say, "put on some real clothes before they come back."

"Yes, Dad." Tabitha's tone is sarcastic. She's unused to being parented. I smile and squeeze my daughter's hand. "Now say your goodbyes."

Kidogo has been churning up a storm in the sink. She's already made projectiles of the paper towel dispenser and the plastic drain board, and now she's applauding by smacking two Brillo pads together. The baboon snorts merrily. Tabitha lift her out of the sink by the armpits.

"Should I pack some toys for her?" asks Tabitha.

"They have toys in Cuba."

"Just a few," says Tabitha. "For the trip."

My daughter darts to the porch. She returns with several fluorescent rings, a rubber pumpkin, a stringy velvet orangutan. Meanwhile, I retrieve my own supplies: my spare gardening gloves, a handful of mangoes, a bottle of valium. I use one of the mangoes to lure the baboon down to the garage and into the trunk of the Saturn.

"It'll just be for few minutes," I apologize. "She'll have plenty of air."

Tabitha leans into the trunk. She rubs noses with Kidogo, scratches the sensitive skin behind her ears. "I'll love you always," she says. "I promise."

My daughter draws back her head. I slam the trunk lid like a guillotine.

We stand inches apart in the hot stillness of the garage. Around us rest the relics of Tabitha's childhood: a warped ping-pong table folded on its side, a pogo stick, an iron cabinet stocked with board games, the husks of several cardboard dioramas. There are also dented metal trashcans, Annie's easel. The air smells of mulch. And now a three-year-old Saturn sedan with a baboon locked in its trunk. Until I drive away. I guess that's what happens to all childhoods. They're carted away, piece by piece, until nothing remains.

"One thing," I say. "About your companions in crime. Rabbits and rats. They won't break down and confess, will they?"

Tabitha cast her eyes toward the floor. She shakes her head.

"You sure, Tabby?"

"I didn't have any companions," she says. Her voice is hardly audible. "I let the rabbits and rats out in the park. It was the best I could do."

"You mean you did this on your own?"

"I read about the experiments on-line. I had to do something."

"On your own," I say again.

"You're going to kill me, aren't you?"

I place my thumb under her chin and raise her head. "I love you, Tabby," I say. "Far more than you love that baboon. Never forget that."

"Make sure she's safe."

"I will," I promise. "Now clean up the house. We'll have plenty of time later to discuss your life of crime."

Tabby smiles.

I press the garage door opener, flooding us with sunlight. I wave at my daughter as I pull the Saturn down the driveway. I've never been so proud of her in my life.

It's around 4:30 pm when I arrive at the Pelican Cove Marina. The attendant, Ike, is a jovial retiree with a full white beard. He knows me well. Several years ago, I helped get his granddaughter admitted to the state university at Gainesville, so when he hears that I've planned a romantic surprise for Francine—an unqualified fabrication—he's delighted to loan me the spare keys to her speedboat. So far, so good. I pull the *King Woody II* out into the channel. A shirtless teenager is feeding mackerel to the cormorants on a nearby jetty. The fat birds squawk and tussle over fish. Already, the sun is dipping toward a pink horizon, playing cat-and-mouse with a bank of innocent clouds. When I clear the harbor, I open the throttle and hug the mangroves until I reach a thoroughly secluded patch of sand. It's an abandoned loading dock at the end of a lane of ground seashells. That's where I've left the Saturn. That's where Kidogo waits for me.

I pop the trunk. The baboon peers tentatively over the side, her eyes adjusting to the blinding light. When she sees me approaching, she bellows a series of high-pitched chirps. This is a good sign. The equivalent of tail-wagging in dogs.

"None of that," I warn her. "We'll have to gag you."

She jumps into my arms and snuggles her nose against mine. Within minutes, we're out on the open water.

To the south lies Cuba. Three hundred miles. To the west is open water, the Dry Tortugas, Mexico. "I'm going to miss you, you dumb baboon."

My eyes are tearing up. Kidogo frowns in sympathy.

"You have to understand," I explain. "It's nothing personal." We are soon out of sight of the shoreline, cruising fast. "I have no choice," I add. *I don't have a choice.* I've thought it all through. Calling Francine isn't an option—I understand that now. She has her own priorities. She'd want no part of this. And Cuba? Far too much risk. I'd get caught. And how could I possibly explain smuggling this baboon out of Florida in a way that wouldn't implicate Tabitha? That wouldn't threaten her future?

"I'm not happy with my decision," I say. "But I can live with it." I feed Kidogo one final mango, slice by slice. I've taken care to embed a handful of valium in the fruit. She drifts off to sleep with the dusk. I slide my hands into my gardening gloves and firmly close them around her throat.

Gelada baboons are native to the Horn of Africa. Although Darwin discusses them in the *Origin of Species*, he relies upon first-hand observations of other naturalists. His own research focuses on finches, tortoises, and mockingbirds. These he gathers, week after week, while the Beagle island-hops through the Galapagos. He does not yet recognize that different species inhabited different islands. He stores his specimens together, unmarked, in one large bag. The significance of the finches' beaks, some blunt, some stout, some pointy, is, for the moment, entirely lost upon him.

The winter the Beagle leaves London, Charles Darwin is only twenty. That's my daughter's age. Years will pass before he figures out what's important.

Enoch Arden's One Night Stands

The Pelican City Young Widows & Widowers Bereavement Circle met every Tuesday evening in the art/music/dance room of the Pelican Harbor Jewish Day School. The room itself was cluttered with the odd chaff of children's festivity: stacks of miniature xylophones, a pink tutu abandoned on an old gymnastics mat, finger paintings suspended along a line like laundry. Alex—who had arrived nearly an hour early—did not wish to be the first to cross the threshold. Instead he waited outside in the underlit corridor. Here the walls had been painted a cloying institutional yellow. Glass cases ran along both sides of the passageway, one documenting the history of the Holocaust through photography and the other relating local efforts to rehabilitate injured manatees, the parallel displays reflecting the heaped carcasses of Mauthausen and Ravensbrück onto newspaper images of beached aquatic fauna. Alex paced the length of the manatee exhibit, skimming the articles from the *Harbor Gazette* with nervous indifference, before suddenly latching onto the dangers of aiding sea mammals: That's how Karen had died, he decided. It was as promising a lie as any.

Although he'd had twenty-six months to decide precisely what had killed Karen, Alex had only given it meaningful thought in the five weeks since Big Mitch suggested a support group. "It's not just about what it's about, boss," the one-armed sous-chef had prodded him. "When I was in NA, nobody went to get clean. Half the women there were there for cock," he added. "And the other half were there for pussy." Maybe, thought Alex. But you couldn't show up for grief counseling if your spouse was still alive, he knew, so he imagined ways to kill her off: *My wife was devoured by alligators. My wife was kidnapped by pirates. My wife was vaporized by pioneers from the Andromeda Galaxy.* He strove to keep the scenarios as implausible as possible—to avoid all thought of serial rapists and ocean undertows—and in the end he was back at square zero. So why not death by sea cow? He'd say that Karen had detoured from her after-noon jog to comfort a stranded manatee, and the creature had dragged her off to Davey Jones' locker. He'd say....

Alex's eyes grew moist; he dared not wipe them. People passed behind him in the corridor—beneath the Israeli flag and into the room with the undersized chairs attached to undersized desks. Alex did not look up. His entire body rebelled against these first awkward moments of know-ing nobody, enflaming his forehead, flushing the tips of his ears, so he did what he often did at weddings and parties: He focused all of his earthly attention on the first inanimate object to cross his gaze, which in this case happened to be the final glass panel in the manatee display. Staring back at him—all of her earthly attention focused on the Holocaust photographs to his rear—shone the petrified dark eyes of a young female reflection.

Causes of death, it turned out, played little role in group bereavement. The widows and widowers did not gather in a conclave and introduce them-selves like alcoholics: *My name is John, I'm thirty-five, my wife toppled off a Ferris wheel; I'm Mary, forty-two, my husband skimped on second-rate fugu.* While the facilitator, Charlotte Ann, spoke at some length about the three drunk teenagers who'd shattered her husband's canoe with their speedboat, the other survivors—Will, Natalie, T.J., Tina, G-Man, Sammy B. and Joanna—steered clear of the morbid. They told stories of ski trips and tailgate parties; they complained about delinquent babysitters and the awkward prospect of introducing a new girlfriend to old in-laws. Alex grew anxious for each speaker. He wanted them to go over well—for their sakes. When it came time for the delicate, dark-eyed girl named Joanna to unburden herself, he thought of her reflection and how he had looked away too suddenly, and now he positively trembled. It was her first meeting too. She told of how her husband had once been clawed by a cat at his office on the afternoon before a charity dinner-dance, and how that evening when she accompanied him into the unisex restroom at the Cormorant Arms hotel to change the dressings on his wounds, the door jammed shut behind them. "So I manage to tear my gown practically in half, working on the lock," said Joanna. "And I'm shouting. And I'm crying. Help me! Let me out! The whole nine yards. When the security guy finally gets the door open, there I am with the front of my dress ripped open and Owen sitting on the toilet seat with his shirt off and scratch marks all over his chest and neck." The girl spoke very quickly, in desperate bursts. She couldn't have been more than twenty-five. When she finished her story, Alex realized that he was smiling directly at her.

Charlotte Ann thanked Joanna. Others murmured assent. "Anyone else?" asked the facilitator.

Everyone except for Alex had spoken. He looked down at the top of his miniature desk. A choppy hand had scrawled on the wood: *Why couldn't Helen Keller drive? Because she was a woman. Why couldn't Helen Keller read? Because she was from Alabama.* She'll adjourn the meeting, Alex thought, and I'll never come back. Nearby, the equine woman named Natalie reached for the jacket on the back of her chair.

"*That* man," chirped Joanna. "He hasn't had a chance."

Alex suddenly found himself at stage center.

Charlotte Ann grinned. "Would *that man* like a chance?" she asked.

"Sure," lied Alex. "Why not?" And then he told the story of the night he'd proposed to Karen—when they were both only eighteen and living up north in Trenton, New Jersey. Her stepfather had owned a downtown bowling alley. Alex worked there as the manager on weekend evenings. During the pre-dawn darkness, the deserted Capital Lanes were an ideal setting for a lovers' tryst. Every Saturday night for nearly a year, Alex drove his future father-in-law home—and as soon as the old man entered the house, his daughter snuck out of the shrubbery for the return trip to the sofa in the bowlarama office. Until the March of their senior year. On the final day of that month, a Sunday, a mini-blizzard swept through Trenton after midnight. It's heavy, wet snow clung to the burgeoning leaves like webbing. When Alex and Karen arrived at the bowling alley for their rendezvous, a robust white oak had already plummeted through both the roof and the ceiling. Drifts rose waist-high on the lanes around the tree; frost seeped its way along the metal gutters like blood. The automatic pin setters had also gone haywire, toppling and replacing in a berserk game of chicken and egg. Alex was about to phone his employer when Karen's first snowball hit him smack between the eyes, and soon the two of them were on the slick floor of lane seven, groping and giggling, planning a wedding and a honeymoon in Florida. "I miss her," said Alex. "You know."

"Of course, honey," said Charlotte Ann. "We know."

Alex looked over at Joanna to see how his story had gone over, but she was diligently scribbling in a notebook. He tried to delay his own exit. He sat back down again and wrote on his desk: *Why couldn't Helen Keller find a husband?* Alex didn't know exactly why he was waiting, what he was waiting for. Soon he and the delicate girl were the only two people left in the room. When she shut her notebook, she appeared startled to find him still in his seat.

"Oh goodness," she said. "I'm so sorry. About before."

Alex thought back to the reflection in the glass.

"You didn't want to say anything, did you? I realized that as soon as I said something. I'm stupid that way—I was just writing about it in my journal."

"No big deal," said Alex. He didn't like the expression *stupid that way*; he suddenly felt disappointed, almost betrayed.

"What you said was so romantic, though. All that snow reminded me of *Ethan Frome*."

Alex walked her to the elevator and they rode down the three stories in silence. It was only nine o'clock and the summer dusk greeted them on the boardwalk outside. Silhouettes of wood storks crisscrossed the horizon. Alex searched for words to continue the conversation.

"It's a book," said Joanna. "You're wondering about *Ethan Frome*. It's a book, not a movie."

"Okay."

"I'm an English teacher," added Joanna.

"Okay."

Alex focused on two small green lizards darting along the wooden planks. Across the school parking lot, a pickup truck churned dust in its wake.

"I need to unwind after that," said Joanna. "Do you know a good place to eat?"

The lizards ducked under the railing. "You're in luck," said Alex, smiling, relaxing. "I own a restaurant."

"Is it good?"

Nobody had ever asked that before. It was like asking if he was good in bed.

"Not without Karen," he answered, mechanically. "Not any more."

Alex revealed his secret over a sizzling platter of Apalachicola oysters and mussels mariniere. They were ensconced at one of the corner booths in the Quarterdeck Room, swaddled by antique barometers and mollusk-draped rigging. The early bird crowd had long since departed, and through the swinging doors to the kitchen resounded the clash and clatter of the Captain's Mast readying for slumber. "A good restaurant needs beauty sleep, coddling," he said. "When we first bought this place from Karen's aunt and uncle, we tried to run it late into the night. We learned the hard way: The best bistros eat breakfast in bed." Alex refilled his wine glass, conscious of his tongue growing loose in his mouth. "I'm boring you to tears, aren't I?"

"No," answered the girl. "Not particularly."

Alex fumbled with his napkin ring. He regretted his vignette on the history of Oysters Rockefeller—but what else was he supposed to say? Seafood and Karen were the only two things he knew anything about.

A thin smile trailed across Joanna's lips, then faded. "That was supposed to be a joke," she said too quickly. *"The not particularly."*

Alex nodded. "My wife's not dead."

He braced for anger—Karen's temper would have flared. Joanna merely dabbed her lips with her napkin and waited for more.

"She's missing," he said. "Vanished off the face of the earth."

Joanna toyed with her wedding ring; he wondered if this meant something.

"One day she went out jogging" he continued, "and she jogged straight off into oblivion. They had search teams combing the beach for weeks, but nothing. Not so much as a tennis shoe." When Joanna said nothing—just focused on him with her intense, sooty eyes—he let himself go. He spoke of the days squandered leafleting shopping malls, the exertions whose eventual purpose grew merely to fend off suspicion. And he spoke of the uncertainty, the frustrations, the second-guessing. How could he know whether she'd been carried away, gouging and clawing, or absconded fully of her own volition? How did he know if she'd show up again one day—at fifty? At eighty? He read in the paper about missing schoolgirls escaping from cults, amnesiacs stumbling upon long lost spouses, Japanese kidnapees returning from North Korea. All this hope made his bed feel colder, his plight more desperate and urgent. "Every time I accept that she might be dead, something reminds me that she's still alive.... But when I get to thinking she's coming back, death throws me a zinger." Alex tore the top off a pack of artificial sweetener and poured the grains into his water glass, watching them form a sheet of frost on the surface. "Sometimes I dream of footprints on sand," he said. "Shallow footprints filling with murky water."

Joanna reached forward as though to take his hand, but she stopped, tentatively, several inches short. "How awful. Like Enoch Arden."

Alex nodded. "You mentioned that earlier."

"Did I?" puzzled the delicate girl. "Oh, no. That was *Ethan Frome*. This is Enoch Arden. It's a poem by Alfred Lord Tennyson."

"Next time around," said Alex, "I'll go to college."

"It's about this woman, Annie, whose husband is shipwrecked at sea," continued Joanna. "And presumed dead. Only he's actually not dead— and he comes back to find her married to a new man—"

"—named Enoch Arden—"

"—*named* Philip Ray. It's one of those popular misconceptions that the new husband is named Enoch Arden. The *old husband* was named Enoch Arden. Sort of like how some people think the one-armed man was The Fugitive."

Alex stirred the saccharine frosting in his water glass. "Okay," he agreed.

"But here's the important part," said Joanna—her face suddenly aglow like a schoolgirl with gossip. "Enoch doesn't reveal himself to Annie. He loves her too much to ruin her happiness, so he conceals himself in a boarding house and dies alone."

The room turned silent. From the kitchen came the sound of Big Mitch hurling profanities at the industrial dishwasher. "So you're saying that Karen's out there somewhere. Hiding."

The delicate girl wilted. "I don't know what I'm saying," she said, un-moored. "You should read it."

"If I should, then I will." He reached across the table to fill his wine glass one last time. The thought crossed his mind that he had revealed too much and she too little. Good clams enter the pot closed and exit open. His instincts told him that the same rule applied to women and dinner. "And what about you? What's your story?"

"My story?" The delicate girl flicked back her long sable hair. "My story," she announced with sudden decision, "is that it's nearly eleven thirty and I'm teaching *Anna Karenina* tomorrow at eight."

"That's a book," said Alex, grinning. "Not a person."

She stood up and walked briskly toward the door.

"Next week," said Joanna.

Alex agreed—though he wasn't certain what he was agreeing to. "Next week."

That night he missed Karen more than he had in months. Her absence actually afflicted him as physical pain, as a jab somewhere deep within his skull. Ever since losing his wife, Alex had abandoned their queen-size bed. He slept on the moth-gnawed olive sofa in the living room—to hear the door chime, in case she returned in the dark without keys. The couch itself was a stunted little pallet that Karen had once tagged a love-seat with ambitions. It didn't even let him stretch his legs. Yet now, for the first time, this constricted berth struck Alex as far too roomy, and he pitched about on the cushions for hours like a toy boat lost at sea. Shortly after three a.m., he retreated to the lanai. He sat at the end of a dew-soaked chaise longue. He wore only boxer shorts. The breeze off the ocean sent chills down his spine. In the pine barrens that rose beyond the bougainvillea hedge, scarlet ibises roosted like Christmas ornaments. So many of his nights with Karen had been spent in this little nook of paradise—reveling in the shock of their own successes. He could still hear her boasting, her voice slurred with sherry, "*The fucking* American dream!" That was the bare-knuckles Karen speaking, the hardscrabble New Jersey schoolgirl. She was the cart that drove the horse. Alex could not imagine loving anybody different.

When dawn broke, Alex went to market. Karen's uncle had taught him to inspect each fish individually at the wholesalers—to hand-pick the largest pompano, the tilapia and grouper still flailing in the stalls. The work required sharp eyes, stamina. Sometimes a thick apron. Not surprisingly, his arrival at the two-room municipal library several hours later—his work boots and dungarees still lacquered in snook guts—drew the attention of the puffy, chinless young man behind the counter. The youth folded his stubby arms across his breast. "Need any help?"

"Just looking," muttered Alex. Libraries and bookstores generally made him feel self-conscious, and this attendant's polite offer stung like an accusation of shop-lifting. The problem was he'd forgotten the poet's name. He had no choice. He walked briskly to the main desk. "Do you have Enoch Arden?"

The librarian looked up from a crossword puzzle. "Is that a book or an author?"

"It's a poem," retorted Alex. "I don't know who wrote it."

He waited for the librarian to snicker, but the young man merely smiled in sympathy. "That's hard, if you don't know the poet's name."

"It's a famous poem," said Alex.

The librarian scratched the pink flesh around his collar. "You know what I'll do," he said. "I'll phone my grandmother." The youth flicked open his cellular phone, adding in a more professional voice: "She reads a lot."

They finally found *Tennyson—Selected Poems* in the children's room; it had been propped against one of the windows to keep the air-conditioner from blowing open the drapes.

The delicate woman didn't show up the following week, or the next. Alex had arrived early both evenings in the hope of discussing Enoch and Philip and Annie Lee. He'd also tackled "In Memoriam" and "The Charge of the Light Brigade"—the idea of knowing something other than shellfish *did* appeal to him—but it was Arden's turmoil that he burned to explore. She'd said next week, hadn't she? A promise, a contract. What sort of person plays so fast and loose with her words? Alex understood that he had no legitimate gripe against the woman—she'd made an idle remark to a virtual stranger, nothing more—but he didn't care. So what if his anger was irrational? Anger wasn't rational. On the occasion of Joanna's second absence, Alex shared the Enoch Arden tale with the rest of the support group. Philip Ray, the second husband, sent Sammy B. into a dither. His own dead wife, it turned out, had been unfaithful. G-Man called Enoch a "chicken-shit bastard" who deserved what he got. When Tina stood up for the hapless fisherman—"it's just like on *The Days of Our Lives*," she insisted—the two went at each other's throats. Eventually, they both turned on Alex. He apologized: "It was stupid to bring up." For the remainder of the meeting, he kept silent. His attention drifted, and he counted the colored tags that labeled the walls, the windows, the chalkboard in both Hebrew and transliterated English. He read the wisdom on his desktop: *Abe Lincoln was Jewish. He was shot in the temple.* Also: *Lucy eats snotburgers, Chazz & Lindsay 4ever.* In response to *Why couldn't Helen Keller find a husband?* someone had inked *Because she was a lesbian.* Alex snuck a glance at his watch. At the Captain's Mast, Big Mitch would be rolling out the first of the key lime pie.

I'm not coming back, he decided. Enough is enough.

He did, of course. He arrived early again—planning to ask the facilitator if she knew the delicate woman's last name, seething with two week's pent up frustrations—to discover Joanna standing in the corridor and sipping coffee from a Styrofoam cup. She wore a low-cut cotton dress. The fine ridges of her collarbone danced with every breath. Alex examined her reflection in the glass display case—where a tribute to Israeli astronaut Ilan Ramon had replaced the manatee exhibit. Everything about her struck him as so fragile, almost ethereal: her slender shoulders, her perfect teeth aligned like small white tombstones. A contrast to his wife's substance, fullness—to Karen's fleshy thighs and the breasts he could palm like baby pumpkins. In the glass, he traced Joanna's fine features—superimposed upon a profile of the space shuttle at dawn, reflecting also the death chamber atrocities and swastika-emblazoned banners from the opposing glass case—to uncover his own reflection, and her eyes once again locked upon his. He shifted his gaze to the fringes of the Shuttle Columbia portrait and examined them with a sudden and ferocious intensity. She reeled to face him, leaving his eyes no escape.

"You're back," she said. "I'm so glad."

His anger—what was left of it—turned upon him. All of his past frustrations now seemed so unreasonable, so utterly overblown. "I read the poem," he said.

The threads of her eyebrows rose in uncertainty.

"Enoch Arden," said Alex. "I wanted to tell you how much I enjoyed it, but you weren't here...."

"Oh, Tennyson," answered Joanna. "I'm so glad you liked it. Many people don't, you know."

Alex tucked his thumbs into the pockets of his slacks. It hadn't crossed his mind that G-Man and Sammy B. were in the majority—that *he* was the odd man out. "I don't know much about poems," he said. "All I know is what I like."

Joanna nodded. "Some people find Arden a bit too...forced, maybe hackneyed. All that Victorian gloom and doom. I like to think Enoch must have had a mistress tucked away somewhere, maybe more than one...." The woman paused, bit her lip. She added disdainfully: "Tennyson would never tell us that, of course."

"Of course," echoed Alex.

He followed her into the meeting room. His entire understanding of the poem had suddenly come loose at the hinges—and all the questions he'd had for the delicate woman no longer seemed relevant. After Karen's disappearance, Alex had seriously wondered whether she might have been having an affair. How could he not? Yet if that were the case—and deep down he didn't accept it—then he'd always assumed the transgression and her absence to be linked. Either she'd run off with this unknown man, or he'd done to her the unspeakable. A third possibility now confronted him: Maybe his wife had been unfaithful *independent* of her disappearance. Everybody had secrets, after all. One look around the circle at his grief-stricken companions—all of whom except Joanna and Charlotte Ann had already confessed to cheating—reminded him how easy it must be to become enmeshed in the tangled gossamer of infidelity.

Joanna told the circle about her trip with Owen to the Galapagos—of how they'd watched the mating dances of the blue-footed boobies and how her husband had tried to replicate them in their cabin. Alex didn't reveal anything. He waited for her at the end of the meeting, but the equine woman named Natalie had visited the ladies' room, and now shared their elevator ride. Natalie also had a connection to the Galapagos, having watched a Discover Channel special. She peppered Joanna with inanities about giant tortoises and tropical penguins. Mercifully, the woman's ride awaited her at the curbside. Without warning, Alex and Joanna stood alone. The insect lamp drove their long shadows toward the cusp of oblivion.

"You weren't here last week," said Alex.

Joanna held her hands clasped in front of her.

"I had a good time at dinner," she said. "I wasn't ready for that."

Alex rustled in his pocket for his keys. "The mussels were tender, weren't they?"

Joanna smiled. "Passable," she said.

She nodded in the direction of the beach—and they walked down the boardwalk, alongside the cast-iron benches and topiary shrubs. Beyond the grassy dunes, the distant surf murmured through the darkness. "Do you want to know?" she asked.

"I wouldn't have asked."

"Owen drove off the Cormorant Island causeway," she said.

"Intentionally?"

Joanna shrugged her frail shoulders. "Who knows? He was a pediatric dentist.... One of the girls said things....said he did things....."

"Oh Jesus," said Alex. "Was it....?"

"How the hell should I know?" slashed Joanna. "She was goddam *thirteen*."

She paused and drew in her breath; she made no effort to dampen her tears. "I'm sorry. You didn't deserve that." The young woman stretched her arms, opening her hands as though to cast away anger like feed grain. "Uncertainty," she said.

"You're telling me," answered Alex. "Dinner?"

Her nod was faint, fleeting—yet it was a nod. And over dinner they discussed lighter topics: the rare yellow lobster on display at the Tampa aquarium, the ongoing boycott of sea bass and bluefin tuna. Joanna had her own take on shellfish: She related how Cleopatra had dissolved a pearl earring in wine to prove Egypt's wealth to Marc Antony, how Chekhov had written of oysters, and later how the playwright's coffin had been transported from Germany to Moscow on a freight car labeled "For Oysters Only." She also spoke of her interest in poetry. She'd arrived at literature "late in life"—she'd actually studied marine biology in college, but had killed time reading while waiting for "scientific magic" in the lab—and, at the end of the evening, she even recited Browning's "My Last Duchess" to the delight of the kitchen staff.

"Encore," demanded the one-armed sous-chef. "Encore"

"Next week," she promised—to Alex, to Big Mitch, to the twin busgirls Susana and Mariana. "You've worn me out."

She stopped Alex from walking her to her car: "Next week."

When he returned to the kitchen—half jubilant, half on-edge—Big Mitch cut the ground out from under him. "She isn't nothing like Karen," he said. "Not better or worse, you know. Just a different cut of meat."

"How do you break up with someone you're not dating?" Alex asked Big Mitch.

They were standing on either side of the seafood station, shucking oysters. Alex had already jabbed himself twice. A few stray shells lay in a puddle of bloody water on the countertop. Alex admired Big Mitch's dexterity. The sous-chef held each oyster in his one large hand—and carved it with a thick makeshift blade strapped to his thumb.

"Fucking depends," said Big Mitch. "You breaking up with her to start dating her? Or you breaking up to get rid of her?"

Alex stuck his knife into the wooden cutting board. He dabbed horseradish on a raw oyster and sucked the tiny body into his mouth. "Good flavor in these Olympias," he said. "Try one."

"Not in May," said the sous-chef. The conventional wisdom—long since trumped by commercial farming—warned against oysters in months whose names did not contain the letter "r". The sous-chef carried his cache of mollusks to the shellfish refrigerator. "Nothing romantic about getting the runs."

"I don't know what I want," said Alex. "She didn't show up again last week. That's four meetings out of the last seven."

The sous-chef returned and carried off Alex's store of oysters. "Why the fuck don't you just ask her out? Take her dancing or something?"

"Jesus Christ," said Alex. "I'm married."

The sous-chef shrugged his one good shoulder. "Don't stop most people," he said. "And if you're so married, boss, where's your wife at?"

The ceiling fan buzzed overhead like a helicopter. Big Mitch stepped into the alcove bathroom and left the door open; Alex heard his urine hitting the water. "You're way out of line," shouted Alex.

The toilet flushed; the faucet ran. "So fucking fire me," called the sous-chef. He returned with the fronds of his hawaiian shirt poking through his fly.

They glared at each other: Alex's eyes flashed sharp and hot against Big Mitch's unflappable durability. The sous-chef's exposed stump—a birth defect, not a war injury—suggested courage, street smarts. Eventually, Alex looked away. His gaze settled on a shiny silver pot brimming with crushed ice.

"It's me I should fire," he said. "How about bowling?"

The enterprise proved far easier than Alex had anticipated. He offered; she accepted. That evening—after a raucous meeting in which Sammy B. publicly declared his love for an unsuspecting Tina—they braved a torrential Gulf Coast squall, which had flooded shut the interstate, and followed the mangrove-lined back roads to Sawgrass Bowling & Billiards. Joanna drove: a beige Dodge Dart from the late 1970's that resembled a giant cigar on roller skates. The car's interior smelled of spearmint, of lemongrass, of woman's shampoo. Hand-knit hoods covered the seat backs; baby pink Mardi Gras beads dangled from the overhead light. Magazine clippings—cartoons, photographs—were scotch taped to the face of the dashboard. Alex's father, a transmission specialist from Camden, always insisted that cars mirrored souls. That theory made Joanna spiritual, complicated. Alex's own pickup stank pungently of ocean musk—evaporated brine, mackerel viscera—which also struck him as an unfortunate confirmation of his father's hypothesis.

"When was the last time you went bowling?" asked Alex.

"You'll laugh," answered Joanna. "I've never been."

"Never?"

Joanna squinted through the sheets of rain. "Owen had a bad knee. He fell off a horse as a kid." Something inchoate and feral cut across the road; Alex's foot reached for an imaginary brake. "It's amazing, you know, how people define each other. *Owen* had a bad knee, so *I* never went bowling."

"With Karen it was airplanes," said Alex. "Scared the living shit out of her."

His own use of the past tense caught him off guard.

"I love flying," said Joanna. "It's like magic."

The glowing, low-slung form of the Sawgrass Lanes rose suddenly against the gray horizon. A sign out front flashed "OWL" "OWL" "OWL" in neon—the burned out "B" hunkered down against the storm. If Karen's father was running the place, thought Alex, he'd have me out there changing bulbs in a hurricane. But the old man was dead, of course. Diabetes. Renal failure. Too independent, too stubborn, for dialysis. Yet the interior of the Sawgrass Lanes—that septic junior high school stench, poorly lacquered over with cleanser and verbena—pricked at Alex's memory. A list of 300 game bowlers ran the height of one wall; a case of league trophies traversed the length of another. In the far corner, near a decapitated payphone, teenagers clustered around an arcade game. Somewhere out of view, Alex sensed, hid a manager's office with a sofa.

"What do we do first?" asked Joanna. "You've got to tell me what to do, you know. I don't want to mess up."

Alex steered them to the shoe-exchange counter. Thunder from outside melded with the crash of falling pins. "There's only one important rule in bowling," he said. "You want to make sure you keep the ball on your own lane."

"Like driving," said Joanna.

"You've got it," said Alex. "I've never thought of that."

Joanna examined her bowling shoes suspiciously; they were the smallest size. "You'll teach me step by step?" she asked.

"I promise. Just like swimming."

They were already through nine frames—with Alex leading 186 to 47—when the conversation rapidly veered away from bowling. It was all Alex's doing, though he wasn't sure what prompted him. Maybe the 50's music, maybe the college kids on a double date in the adjacent lane. "Those poets," he said, apropos of nothing. "Browning. Tennyson. Swinburne. They must have gotten lonely."

Joanna sat down beside him on the plastic aqua bench. She held her bowling ball between her legs, as though she'd just given birth to a boulder. "Swinburne?"

Alex had discovered Swinburne on his own; he now feared that he'd pronounced the poet's name incorrectly. "What I mean is—it must get lonely doing all that writing."

"I always think it's worse for the characters," answered Joanna. "They're stuck forever in the same bad relationships. Poor Hester, poor Anna. But sometimes I think it's all a pack of lies—that Emma Bovary was actually messing around with Homais the chemist."

"Yes," agreed Alex. ""Or that Enoch Arden was having one night stands."

Immediately they both realized that they were no longer talking about what they were talking about. Joanna fumbled with the gold bangles around her wrists; sometime since their first meeting, Alex realized, she'd removed her wedding band. He glanced nervously around the alley. Most of the other lanes stood empty. One of the college couples had departed early, while the other had given up bowling. The girl now sat on the guy's lap—and he clearly had his hand under her skirt. Women inside, Alex remembered, feel like squid.

"There's a scene in *Anna Karenina*," said the delicate woman in a wispy voice, "in which this learned intellectual named Sergey Ivanovitch and a poor relation named Varenka go out mushroom picking...."

Alex's lower back had started to cramp—too much bending—but he dared not stretch. From the seat behind them came the desperate sounds of giggling or whimpering; he focused hard on Joanna.

"....They have this moment," she continued. "Out in the forest. Where either he'll propose—where something will happen between them, or it will all be over forever...."

Joanna looked up; a thin smile traced her trembling lips.

Alex felt his own body fluttering. He knew something was called for—statement, action. A charge of urgency swept through him, priming his senses, magnifying the odor of floor polish and the clatter of pins. But with his heightened emotions came the sudden tug of the past—flashing before him that lost moment of youthful enrapture on lane seven, the groping, the fumbling, Karen's long auburn hair dappled with frost. He could feel her snow-numb nose meeting his—like Eskimos. The memory reached for him like a hand reaching forth from the grave. Alex found his focus entirely derailed and he stared blankly at Joanna. Her eyes remained wide and hopeful. She was waiting for him to speak.

"*Anna Karenina*," Alex said finally. "I've never read it." He struggled for something further and added: "Is it good?"

Joanna opened her mouth to answer, but didn't. Across the alley came a ripple of plangent euphoria—someone had toppled his tenth straight strike. Alex watched the fellow high-fiving his buddies.

"Yes, of course," said Joanna sharply. "It's good."

She stood up and walked rapidly to the ladies' room. After that, they bowled out the last frame, speaking only when necessary, and she drove him home.

The storm worsened past midnight. The wind picked up something fierce, slashing palm branches against the siding of the bungalow. Alex sat on the edge of the threadbare couch in his boxer shorts. He wanted something to happen—he wanted the doorbell to ring. "Ring the goddam bell," he thought. "Just ring the goddam bell!" Whether he was speaking to his missing wife, or to the delicate woman, even he no longer knew. Around three a.m.—shortly after the power went dead—he lit a candle and read to himself the opening passages of *Enoch Arden*. He grew drowsy. The words waltzed aimlessly under the lambent flame. Alex kept waiting, irrationally, for Enoch to reveal himself to his wife. He didn't of course. When the tears came to Alex's eyes, he folded shut the book and retreated to the master bedroom. He slammed shut the door behind him and slept with the thick down comforter pulled snug over his head. It was the deep, stony sleep of a man who'd died twice in one night.

The Ataturk of The Outer Boroughs

Thirty-one year old Onur Erdem was re-keying the tumblers on an antique strongbox when the pretty woman attorney arrived to carry off all that he owned. The Turkish locksmith greeted her warnings with a meditative silence: He gritted his molars down on his calabash pipe and fed a stack of blanks through the computerized code cutter. Twice already he had lost everything—once to the creditors who'd bankrolled his late father's gambling sprees, once to an electrical fire—so the prospect of dispossession, which in the past might have conjured up traumatic images of refugees pulling featherbeds with horse-carts, now merely vexed him like a minor rash. Transience was the price for breathing American air, for doing business in Jackson Heights, Queens. He could live with it. (That was why, in his personal affairs, he favored things British—test match cricket, Darjeeling tea from Taylors of Harrogate—anything that smacked of stability and empire.) Yet Onur enjoyed having the pretty woman attorney, whose name was Claudia Crane and whose sandy hair flaunted an un-lawyerly streak of fuchsia, sitting with her legs crossed on the cast iron mini-vault in his shop. Claudia wore a black skirt, stockings. Pink lacquered nails poked through the toes of her shoes. Onur noticed her wedding ring, but still had no desire to see her leave too quickly. "What did you call it?" he asked.

"Eminent domain," answered Claudia. "If they pay you fair market value, they can come take your property."

Onur nodded indifferently. He blew the tiny brass shavings from each of the processed keys, holding the finished products to the light one at a time. "I understand that," he said. "Why don't you stop them?"

Claudia breathed deeply—maybe to mask frustration. "That's what we're trying to do, but at this point it won't be easy. They already have an order of necessity."

"Why didn't you stop them sooner?" asked Onur. He fancied the way his visitor toyed with her crystal necklace.

"We didn't know. All the state has to do is run 'notice of intent' ads in the local papers, and that's like not doing anything at all. The whole process is completely Kafkaesque. What I mean is—"

"I understand Kafkaesque," said Onur.

Claudia took another deep breath—this time pausing to exhale as though she'd been punched in the abdomen. "*Of course*, you do," she said. "What I wanted to emphasize was that if we don't take action soon, the bulldozers are going to roll over your business."

"And my home," interjected Onur. "I live upstairs."

"*And* your home. *And* my office. *And* the Whatever 4 Cafe. *And* everything else within six square blocks. All in the name of hockey. And minor league hockey at that. All so that a bunch of assholes can get piss drunk, shout obscenities and drive home."

The locksmith smiled thinly; he wished to conceal his jagged teeth. Although he had no interest in hockey, the prospect of a government buyout actually had its plusses: What better excuse to invest in cutting-edge equipment? Or he might expand into home security systems, maybe closed-circuit surveillance. Next year—when the hockey players rolled through—he'd be installing burglar alarms in the suburbs. His aunt might not like the move, but she'd get over it. Onur bit his tongue to keep from laughing, steeled his face. "Is that hockey on grass?" he asked. "Or hockey on ice?"

"Hockey on ice. An arena. Please, Mr. Erdem, we need you."

"Me? *I'm* so important?"

Claudia glanced toward the shop window. Her pale slender neck shimmered like rose marble under the fluorescent light. "I'll be honest with you, Mr. Erdem," she said in a hushed voice. "We think it's very important for the committee to reflect the community...Different viewpoints, you know."

Onur wondered how many Gujarati *farsan* mongers and Senegalese hair beaders and Hmong green grocers the woman attorney had approached before finding him. He explored the stem of his pipe with his tongue, while running security keys across the electric buffer. "Did you know that the first locks were made of wood?" he asked.

The woman attorney smiled at him as though he'd walked in off the moon.

He looked straight into her eyes for the first time. He had a granduncle in Baltimore—also a locksmith—who'd once told him that the eyes were like keyholes into the palaces of royalty. He had been only a child; the uncle had been drinking. Now Onur wondered what regal secrets lurked behind the pretty woman's opaque gray irises. She struck him as a woman of significant complexity. "The first wooden locks adorned the imperial gates of Sargon of Persia in the eighth century before Christ."

"How interesting," said Claudia.

"I think so," said Onur. "You said you wanted diverse viewpoints. I'm offering you the viewpoint of a locksmith."

The woman attorney opened her mouth—but at first no words came out. She finally asked, "Does that mean you'll do it?"

"Sure," he said. "I'll do it."

He shook her hand across the countertop. He did not appreciate the way that she held her arm straight out from her body; it was almost insulting. But her long, glabrous fingers were as cold and delicate as porcelain. Outside, a taxicab honked. Onur relinquished the exquisite tiny hand. His body shivered at the burst of chill air as the woman attorney exited the shop.

On the counter stood a coffee cup. It bore the inscription: "Small keys open large doors"—a present to his late father from a friend. Onur picked up the stack of newly minted keys and dropped them into the cup, one by one. The polished metal clinked on glass like coins upon the stones in a fountain.

"You're running out on me for *that*?" asked Jude Basso.

The twenty-six-year old elevator technician leaned over the chessboard; his beefy forearms rested atop his thighs. Onur had competed against Basso on the Internet for months before discovering that the Italian lived in nearby Flushing. Now the two men played in Onur's sitting room, as they did every Wednesday evening, surrounded by the scents of turmeric and toasted caraway. Mama Fairuza, Onur's maiden aunt, had cleared the tea service moments earlier.

"Trust me," said Onur. He used his palms to mime the shape of the woman attorney's chest. "Like the Himalayas."

Basso shifted his queen's bishop the full length of the chessboard with the assurance of a surgeon wielding a scalpel. "Has her husband invited you mountain climbing?" he asked.

"Come and see for yourself, my friend," said Onur. From the kitchen rose the crunch of Mama Fairuza grinding coriander for Harissa sauce. The locksmith removed Basso's bishop and replaced it with his king's knight. "Checkmate."

"I'm no politician," said Basso. He stared at the chessboard in wonder—as though attempting to Monday morning quarterback a shell game.

"And *I'm* a politician? It's all about business."

Onur explained his calculus to the Italian. If the activists defeated the hockey arena, his stature in the community would rise considerably—and that could only be good for the shop. If the developers prevailed, of course, he'd pocket his 'fair market value' and upgrade to a security outfit on the Island. Neither way could he lose. "So I'll pay lip service to property rights and John Locke and Jefferson," he told the bewildered Italian, "but what I'm *really* doing is marketing *me*."

Basso grinned. "I bet you want to pay lip service."

"We'll tell them you live in my building," said Onur. "It's not like you're doing anything else tonight."

Onur settled the chessboard onto its perch atop the piano. He threw on his black cashmere coat and led Basso down the two flights of steep wooden stairs into the bitter gelid night. They walked quickly, the wind at their backs. The gusts hooked sandwich wrappers around car antennas and sandblasted the traffic signs. It was too cold to speak. When they finally arrived at the offices of Tooth Fairy Orthodontics, where the steering committee conducted its biweekly meetings, tears frosted the corners of Onur's eye sockets. Fifteen people had already crowded into the lobby. He recognized the orthodontist, Dr. Gussoff, from his subway advertisements; Gussoff's rodentine features instilled even less confidence in person. The pretty woman attorney was also present, speaking with the elderly Ismaili Muslim who owned the flower shop at the corner of Jackson Avenue and St. James. All the rest were male and strangers.

"Looks like you've got competition," whispered Basso. The locksmith stood in the doorway defrosting, watching the florist demonstrate a dance move to the female attorney.

"Piss off," answered Onur.

He wove his way through the sea of bodies. The woman attorney had traded her business outfit for tight acid-washed jeans, glossy maroon boots and a skimpy scarlet top. She flashed her smile in his direction—and he was about to call out her name—when a robust older man emerged from the crowd to peck her on the lips. The newcomer wore a thick mustache and had eyebrows like hedgerows. Onur heard Claudia introduce him to the Ismaili. "Mr. Kurji. My husband, Eric."

Onur stepped into their conversation. He did not like that the woman attorney had any husband other than him. "Ms. Crane," he said.

"Ah, Mr. Erdem," said Claudia. "Mr. Kurji was just showing me a traditional Tajik folk dance."

"The dance of the eagle," said the florist. "It is usually accompanied by flutes."

The locksmith did not know any traditional Turkish dances. At the state university, he'd won the intercollegiate waltz competition three years running.

"Who has time for dancing?" asked Onur. "We have a neighborhood to save, don't we?"

He had intended no offense—but the crestfallen Ismaili mumbled apologies, his hands jammed into his trouser pockets and his gaze down at the floor.

"I don't see it that way at all," said Claudia. "I agree with the anarchist Emma Goldmann: If I can't have dancing—traditional dancing, folk dancing—I don't want your revolution." The woman attorney added all too quickly: "But I am glad you've come, Mr. Erdem. We need enthusiasm like yours."

At that moment, the orthodontist rose on a plastic milk crate—like a false muezzin on an ersatz minaret—and called the meeting to order. The woman attorney took her place at Gussoff's side, affording Onur no opportunity to say anything further. The locksmith retreated to the back wall. He tried to feign interest in the speakers—the manager of the Whatever 4 Cafe, the proprietor of a local bridal boutique, an architectural preservationist from some obscure foundation—but they bored him senseless. All anger, indignation. With not an original thought among them, each felt the need to throw in his ten cents. The locksmith didn't dare retrieve a magazine from the end table; instead, he busied himself reading a wall poster that diagrammed the components of braces. Bonded brackets. Rubber bands. Archwires. A vocabulary of appliances as intriguing as those in his own shop. He refocused only when the woman attorney mounted the makeshift proscenium.

"You win," said Jude Basso. "Like the Himalayas."

The top buttons hung open on the woman attorney's blouse. From his angle, Onur could see the magenta frills on her brassiere.

"What we need most right now," she said, "are volunteers."

She spoke about recruitment techniques, door-to-door campaigning. Onur left forty-five minutes later as co-coordinator of fund-raising. He knew as much about fund-raising as he did about dancing the rakkas—but at least he lived in the community. His fellow co-coordinator, Jude Basso, had to take the subway seven stops home.

Onur discovered his gift for political oratory the following Saturday at the loading dock behind Caravan Kabul. The Afghani restaurant was owned by two Iranian brothers, identical twins named Malik and Majid; each sported a full gray beard. Although Onur had assisted them several times in the past—once following a burglary, twice after automobile lockouts—he still couldn't tell them apart. For fund-raising purposes, of course, this didn't matter. While one of the brothers and a frozen produce wholesaler inventoried sacks of vegetables as they came off the back of the dealer's truck, the locksmith stood in the flurrying snow and spoke of property rights. Nearby, a visibly uncomfortable Jude Basso chain-smoked cigarettes.

You ask: What does this have to do with me? I'm no politician. I'm no rabble-rouser. I don't want any trouble. That's why you've come to this great country, America—so you can avoid politics and trouble. At least, that's what I myself believed at first. You're likely thinking what I was thinking: I'll take their 'fair market value' and expand. Upgrade. Maybe move out to the suburbs. But what then? Please hear me out, my friend, small business owner to small business owner. What are you going to do when the government comes after your new restaurant, your new store, your new home? My father picked us up from Anatolia—gave up everything he had back in Turkey. *And why? WHY? I ask you. To move where his property would be protected. Not his right to speak. Or even to pray. No, no, no. His right to make a decent living. A secure living. The Declaration of Independence was originally supposed to say "life, liberty and property"—that's what the pursuit of happiness really is. Without property, there is no stability. Without stability—Revolution! That's why we need to stand up for ourselves.*

Onur placed his hand on the Iranian's thick shoulder; his voice dropped to a confidential lull: *They drove you out of Iran in '79. I know how it was, my friend. I know. But don't let them do it to you a second time. Remember how you swore it would never happen again? Here's your chance.*

The Iranian spit into the snow. He signaled for Onur to follow him into the meat pantry, a small freezer that doubled as an office, where the locksmith waited between dangling rabbit carcasses while his host rummaged through the desk for a checkbook. To Onur's shock, the restauranteur—Malik—wrote out a draft for five hundred dollars. "Here," said the Iranian. "Tell them from me: Go fuck themselves."

Similar success greeted Onur at the Cambodian deli, at the television repair shop operated by the Pakistani with the Bell's Palsy, at the storefront offices of the Hungarian foam rubber supplier. All he had to do was alter the proper nouns: *They drove you out of Czechoslovakia in '39. Out of Cuba in '59. Out of Uganda in '72. Or occasionally he'd add a touch of his own personal history: I've been to college, to the state university at Albany, but did I abandon the neighborhood? Of course I didn't. Would I leave my family? Of course I wouldn't. I take pride in being a locksmith—the same way I imagine you take pride in being a landscaper—a piano tuner—a beautician—a liquor dealer—a masseuse. I cared for my widowed mother until she died—I still support her unmarried sister—the same way I am certain you look after your own. So I am not asking for any more than anybody else gets, my friend. But I am not willing to take any less—and I am certain that you are not either.* Onur made a point of leaving his business card at every office and kiosk and apartment that he and Basso visited. Why not? Considering his efforts, the least he deserved was free advertising. He'd distributed more than eighteen hundred by the end of the month—and also raised nearly a quarter of a million dollars— when the woman attorney paid another visit to his shop.

Onur heard the door chime, but did not look up. He was teaching his sixteen year old cousin, Yusuf Gurkan, how to pick a wafer-tumbler with a tension wrench. "When raking the tumblers, the trick is focus," explained the locksmith. "You put pressure on the sidebar with the steel wire, my boy, and you concentrate." Then Onur caught sight of Claudia and nearly sliced off his thumb.

The woman attorney did not appear to notice the mishap. She was leaning over the countertop, examining his family photographs.

"Who's that man?" asked Claudia.

She pointed to a sepia portrait of a dapper young Zouave in puff-trousers, a short red jacket and a matching fez.

"That's my great-grandfather," answered Onur. "During the Russian War. He later served as chief-of-staff under Ataturk."

"Impressive," said Claudia.

Onur grinned—inadvertently exposing his bad teeth.

Claudia returned his smile. "Is there someplace we can speak?"

The locksmith left his cousin in charge of the shop. He led the woman attorney into the stockroom, pulling the bulb light on with a string.

"So this is your secret lair," she said.

The musty, cedar-lined closet embarrassed Onur. He dusted off space atop a worn steamer trunk for the woman attorney to sit down.

Claudia tucked her skirt beneath her. "It's amazing, what you've been doing."

Onur nodded stupidly. "Thank you."

"The truth is," said Claudia, "I came to apologize. For the Emma Goldmann remark the other night. And for misjudging you. I'm a straight-shooting kind of gal, Mr. Erdem, so I'll say it like it is."

The locksmith leaned forward on his splintered wooden stool.

"You weren't our first choice for the steering committee," said Claudia. "Even three weeks ago, I considered asking Mr. Kurji to take your place. But what you've done since then is, well, just unbelievable."

"Oh *that*," said Onur, disappointed. "Nothing beyond the call of duty."

"The call of duty," she echoed. "That's probably what your great-grandfather would have said. Maybe we'll have to start calling you The Ataturk of Jackson Avenue. Or, better yet, The Ataturk of the Outer Boroughs. It has a ring to it."

Onur said nothing.

"You'd make your great-grandfather proud," said Claudia. "Steve Gussoff's getting thirty, forty calls a day. People wanting to volunteer. People wanting to give more money."

"That's good news," said Onur.

He was sitting so close to Claudia, he could smell her shampoo.

"We're going to win this," said Claudia. *"On The Spot News* is doing a story, maybe Channel 5. And our lawyers—thanks to you, we've got a dream team."

"I thought...."

"No, no," said Claudia. "I do family law. I advocate for abused women."

She stood up and extended her hand—still outstretched rigid like a metal bar.

"May I come bother you again, Mr. Erdem?" she asked.

"It's no bother," said the locksmith.

Call me Onur—he thought, the moment she'd left—*Why didn't I ask her? Call me Onur. Call me Onur. Call me Onur.*

The locksmith redoubled his fund-raising efforts. He no longer had time for chess, for monthly backgammon tournaments with his Staten Island relatives. He delegated increasing authority to his teenage cousins, Yusuf Gurkan and Yusuf Nesim, who practically ran the shop in his absence. His waking hours—often from the crack of dawn through the marrow of the overnight—he passed canvassing the neighborhoods beyond the six square blocks of the impact zone.

You ask: What does this have to do with me? They're building that hockey arena in Jackson Heights, not in Corona. Not on 103rd Street and Northern Boulevard. If anything, you think, all those fans will be good for business. But let me tell you—small business owner to small business owner—that you're fooling yourself. Today it's a hockey rink, my friend, but tomorrow it's a sports complex. Parking lots, luxury hotels. Like Disney World. Let me ask you this: Does a wolf devour only one lamb? If today they take what is mine, surely tomorrow they will take what is yours.

Onur left a business card at every encounter. Yet as his sermons grew more urgent, as he haphazardly quoted Patrick Henry and John Stuart Mill and Burke's *Reflections on the Revolution in France*—to Egyptian cabbies and Ecuadorian grocers who didn't know political philosophy from a hole in the floor, the young locksmith became his own most loyal convert. Absolute property, he decided, made sense. The only thing necessary for the triumph of evil, he warned Jude Basso, is for good men to do nothing. Onur's deep-set black eyes acquired a distant, slightly prophetic gleam. He condemned Lenin and the Queens Borough President in one malignant breath. When Mama Fairuza observed that she didn't see what the fuss was about—*Is it so awful that I should die in the suburbs?*—Onur nearly put her out on the street.

Claudia's visits became a weekly, then daily affair. She updated Onur on their legal progress: evidentiary hearings, preliminary injunctions. Once she brought with her a television crew from a cable access channel; on another occasion, she arrived with two city council members from Brooklyn, both Republicans, who'd wanted the hockey arena for an abandoned switchyard between their districts. Onur quoted for them Irving Kristol and Barry Goldwater. He preferred it most, of course, when Claudia arrived alone. That gave him an excuse to invite her back to the stockroom. Later, they graduated to the parlor where his aunt served them tea. All perfectly innocent, of course. But the locksmith knew by memory every inch of fabric in the woman attorney's wardrobe, what days she visited the hair dresser, which earrings she matched with which shoes—a fashion extravaganza etched indelibly into his heart. His interest transcended the political, but it wasn't as though he viewed his canvassing as an arrow into Claudia's affections. Not at all. Rather, the two causes had grown so intertwined in his hysteria that true happiness depended upon both.

And then one March morning—the ides—the pretty woman attorney and her husband arrived together at his shop.

"It's over, Mr. Erdem," she said. "The whole goddam shebang."

Onur surveyed the husband. He wondered how she could prefer this dopey-looking clod who had eyebrows like black moss and hardly ever spoke.

"Judge Katz tore us to shreds. An air-tight, seven hundred page opinion. The old geezer even refused to stay the order pending appeal. He said, and I quote, it is utterly inconceivable that the plaintiff might ultimately prevail."

The husband shrugged his shoulders, dejected.

"Are you crazy?" demanded Onur. "We can't give up."

"We have no fucking choice, I'm afraid."

Onur snapped shut a bronze padlock. He twinged at the memory of the city marshal dragging his father's furniture to the sidewalk in the pouring rain, of the caustic metallic odor that greeted him after the electrical fire.

"How long do we have?" he asked.

Claudia scowled. "The evictions begin May One."

The locksmith nodded. "Plenty of time."

Onur passed the night of April 30th locking people to inanimate objects. The final eviction notices had already been posted for weeks. They came in various unlikely hues—mauve, chartreuse, vermilion—each affixed with four jabs of a staple gun. They reminded Jude Basso of quarantine warnings in science fiction films. From the Viennese waiter at the Whatever 4 Cafe came a harsher verdict: "Anschluss in Technicolor." Earlier in the day, police—not from the local station, but from distant precincts—had barricaded the cross streets. Outbound traffic, only: an entire community of one-way boulevards. Later uniformed officials had spray-painted bright yellow directions on the sidewalks, letters, numbers, indecipherable shapes, a patois recognized only by bureaucrats and bulldozers. Several families did depart; they loaded their Penskes and U-Hauls in sheepish silence. Others dispatched wizened fathers-in-law and toddlers and nursing mothers to the homes of nearby kin. A few businesses, too, carted off their wares: not just the mega-drugstore and the chain supermarket, but also both Korean newsstands and the Dominican drycleaners. Miraculously, that was all. When dusk settled on the last day of the month, the impact zone still teemed with life. By prior arrangement, the locksmith and his cousins went to work.

The three men set about their task systematically: They started at Washington and Hickory, chaining the orthodontist to a postbox, then worked their way north to the corner of Jackson and St. James. Along the way, they fastened and bolted like madmen. They secured people to awnings, to drainpipes, to bicycle stands. King Gordius of Phrygia, boasted Onur, didn't tie his chariot half so well. They tried, of course, to make the captives as comfortable as possible. Most carried water and reading materials to their posts. Restauranteurs issued pots as makeshift bedpans. But the team's ultimate goal had to be security: this was no cause for plastic handcuffs and slipknots. Onur made certain to secure himself and Claudia on either side of his own front door. The husband—"for the sake of reconnaissance"—had been given a cellular phone and been bolted to the trash dumpsters behind the Greek used car lot. "You're our cavalry," explained Onur. "Our eyes and ears." The locksmith had hardly latched himself into place when the roosters from Wirkowski's Live Poultry greeted the dawn.

"I can't believe you pulled this off, Mr. Erdem," said Claudia.

She was wearing her baby pink tank-top without a brassiere.

"Call me Onur," said the locksmith. "Please."

The woman attorney looked away from him. "I was afraid to ask," she said. "How funny. I'm not usually like that."

A solitary black crow landed on the brim of a nearby trashcan.

"You know, Onur," said Claudia. "You're quite amazing."

"Nothing has happened yet," he said.

"But really," insisted the woman attorney. "I don't know if I'm supposed to say this or not—I don't know much about Turkish conventions—but I think you're one of the most amazing people I've ever met. Sincerely."

Onur waited for her to say more, but she didn't. He retrieved several stones from the nearby sidewalk and lobbed them at the crow. He missed each time. Eventually, no more pebbles remained within reach.

"I love the way you dress," said Onur. "You know that, don't you?"

The woman attorney eyed him for a moment. She smiled—but maybe there was less warmth in her smile; he could not be certain. "No, I had no idea."

The locksmith was eager to say more—he had a whole disquisition prepared, in fact, one that he'd repeated to himself for days—but the arrival of police on motorcycles cut him short. State troopers appeared in their wake, then the Commissioner of Public Works wielding a bullhorn. Even the mayor made an appearance: Hizzoner personally entreated Onur to obey the law. But it was the media that generated the frenzy, the scores of reporters and cameramen and executive producers, the sound trucks and satellite feeds, the big name network anchor who compared the locksmith to Gandhi and Martin Luther King. *No, Ataturk*, Onur corrected him. *I think of myself as the Ataturk of the Outer Boroughs.* The newsman nodded and asked: "Who's that?" Claudia, meanwhile, granted interviews of her own. Other than bathroom breaks, conducted behind the veil of a plastic shower curtain, they had no privacy. Certainly no opportunity for an intimate conversation.

At mid-morning, a phalanx of fire engines rolled in. The glistening red trucks gave the lock-in the carnivalesque atmosphere of a tremendous block party. Shackled to the phone booth at the corner of Hickory and 83rd—and supplied with several dozen rolls of quarters—Jude Basso told the locksmith that the vehicles reminded him of the Italian civil defense drills from his childhood. *More like floats in a private parade*, thought Onur. He relished the flags billowing over the ladders that provided a patriotic, all-American backdrop for his soliloquies on Madisonian democracy. Someone had the good sense to run an extension cord into the corner deli and to set up a row of televisions on the adjacent sidewalk. Onur watched himself on all three networks simultaneously. He regulated the volume by remote control. The sun rose above the Commerce Bank, trailed across Roosevelt Park and descended behind a stand of little-leaf lindens. Nothing else happened.

Around midnight: a false alarm. Basso roused the locksmith out of a half-stupor to report national guardsmen with bolt cutters. They circled his phone booth—but at the first sight of the press, they retreated.

Onur steeled his vigilance. Claudia's eyes soon drifted shut. He let her sleep. Her body shivered in the damp, and Onur dispatched a reporter for a blanket.

—And then it was over.

Fast. Like a Houdini trick. All done.

A woman reporter told him the news. She was down on her knees, the microphone like a club in his face.

"The consortium pulled out," she said. "No arena."

The locksmith drew back. "Do you mean we won?"

"That's what the Associated Press is reporting. How does it feel?"

"Claudia," he shouted. "We won!"

He unlocked himself—a rather intricate process—and went to work on her bolts. When she was completely free, she hugged him. Tight. His chest against hers. He could feel his pulse in his temples.

The woman reporter persisted: "You must be very excited?"

"Of course, we are," said Claudia. "Now we can return to our lives."

"What a relief that must be," agreed the woman reporter. Other reporters, young and energetic, closed in on the locksmith. He watched on the television monitors as they surrounded him. A broad-shouldered black man in a dark blue parka—Onur recognized him as the host of an edgy cable newsmagazine—thrust his way between the locksmith and Claudia. "You must also be relieved, Mr. Erdem," continued the woman reporter. "You must be excited to return to your business.

The locksmith couldn't breathe. "Yes," he said, mechanically. "My business."

"Tell us a bit about it. About being a locksmith."

He tried to answer—to explain his previous existence—but he couldn't. He no longer remembered the life he'd lived then, not really, except that Claudia hadn't been part of it. His entire past seemed suddenly unsalvageable, like a key blank trimmed too close.

"Tell us about your former life," demanded the cable host.

Another reporter barked a question. And then a fourth. Their words didn't register. *My former life*—Onur stepped backwards, but there was no escape—My former life. My former life.

They thrust their ugly black microphones at Onur's mouth, pressing him further back against his storefront, but he said nothing. *For the first time in months, he had nothing to say.* Nothing newsworthy, at least. Did they really want to hear about his former life? About backgammon or test-match cricket? About chess? About Mama Fairuza's second-rate Harissa sauce? Of course they didn't. Who could possibly want to know about surveillance systems and fire-proof safes and locks, mortise locks and cross bolt locks and janus-faced locks, and all the locks that you could spend your entire life jimmying and picking—and still never be free?

Exposure

Wednesdays and Saturdays are my days off at the pharmacy, but Saturdays my wife is off too, so I do my flashing on Wednesday afternoons. In the mornings, I have my weekly rap session with Dr. Quince-Martin. She rents space on a corridor down by the waterfront—opposite a urologist named Littlecock—and, after a bad storm, the entire office suite smells of rotting fish. Dr. Quince-Martin makes a point of revealing nothing about her private life, but I've taken the liberty of looking her up on the Internet: Her husband is Dr. Martin-Quince, also a shrink, and she acted off-off-Broadway between college and medical school. Bit parts, mostly. Uncle Charley's receptionist in *Death of a Salesman*. A servant girl in *Hedda Gabler*. I'm holding this knowledge in reserve. The reality is that I just see Dr. Quince-Martin to keep Dawn off my back. My wife is all into head-shrinking and pill-popping and talk therapy, says it "rewired her neural circuitry" after the miscarriage, though she doesn't seem so different to me. Personally, I find Dr. Quince-Martin horrendously narrow. One time, when I tried to tell her about flashing, her back stiffened like a coffin lid and she advised me of the limits to physician-patient confidentiality in Connecticut. So now we chat about turning forty, and my step-father's chemotherapy, and Dawn's harebrained plan to build an outdoor deck onto the kitchen. I don't mention anything about showing Mrs. Sproul my genitals.

Mrs. Sproul must be in her early eighties by now. When we had her in fifth grade, she already colored her hair an unconvincing shade of chestnut. Two deep wedges grooved the space above her sharp nose, and her small, sagging breasts played second fiddle to her knobby, uneven collarbones. I distinctly remember someone asking her how old she was—and that same someone receiving a severe lecture on decorum. That someone may have been me. I think I may also have asked the other fifth grade teacher, Miss Tillary, how old her colleague was, and I recall she may have answered "one hundred fifty." So while I knew Mrs. Sproul wasn't in her second century, I cannot express the relief I experienced a few weekends ago when I found the listing "L. & W. Sproul" in the New Haven County white pages. Twice, already, my targets have been dead. The first was Annie Jarmiczek, who'd repeatedly turned me down for a date at U. Conn. She'd fallen through ruptured ice while pond skating. And then my ex-boss from when I worked at Methodist Hospital bled out during routine gallbladder surgery. Which is why, after thirty years, there's a certain solace in knowing that Wilma Sproul is waiting for me like a plump goose on Christmas morning.

I took a swing past the Sprouls' place last week. A trial run. It's a second-story garden apartment facing away from the avenue, separated from the commuter rail tracks by a ribbon of parking lot and a towering privet hedge. The basketball court at one end stands rimless and overgrown with ailanthus trees. All of East Bondleigh has taken an economic drubbing during the last few years, and what was once comfortably middleclass is now lilting toward downright sketchy. But I suppose Mrs. Sproul's choices are limited on a suburban teacher's pension. Or maybe she prefers the invigorating loneliness of New England winters to the stifling loneliness of Florida summers. Her husband, L. Sproul, is dead. His name remains in the telephone directory, but he's been replaced on the mailbox lid with a hand-printed: "Mrs. W. Sproul." While I nosed around the vestibule last week, pretending to read the free advertising circulars, a curvy young woman with purple hair and a razor-sharp nose appeared from the outside step and pushed the buzzer for 2K. She had grocery bags propped against her hips, so I helped her with the door. Clearly the granddaughter—you could cut pills in half with those Sproul family noses. But not bad-looking. She might come back today, I realize—some sort of weekly grocery run—so I know I'll have to work rapidly.

At mid-afternoon, the rear parking strip is nearly empty. I ease in beside a colossal trash dumpster. The remnants of someone's tag sale line the curbside: a warped sofa; a string-less ukulele; table lamps and chandeliers in various styles. All of this still sopping from the weekend squall. But there are also a pair of large marble lions—like giant, ferocious bookends—precisely the sort of kitschy garden ornament that Dawn can't ever get enough of. That's my wife for you: All day long preserving colonial farm houses and country churches and God-knows-what, then she comes home and wants to transform our swampy half acre into Versailles on the Old Mill Creek. Usually, I'd do right by her and drag the abandoned statuary into the back of the Plymouth. There's enough polished stone here to make her month. But today, I can actually see Mrs. Sproul through the wispy lavender drapes—relaxing in the sunlight beside the window, her hair now artificially curled, but still *faux*-chestnut—and I know there will be no time for hauling marble. Revenge is a dish that requires undivided attention to serve.

It's a hot, soupy day, so there's no one loitering on the cast-iron benches behind the Sprouls' building. Just a few grackles feeding in the thick grass. I walk quickly, my bathrobe and ski mask in a gym bag under one arm, my gaze firm and fixed forward. The first time I went on a flashing expedition, now nearly eight months ago, I used a trench coat that I'd lifted off a rack at the local barbecue joint. It had a zip-out fleece lining and a concealed breast pouch for carrying a wallet or a passport. But it made me feel a bit like Dick Tracy. Or even something of a pervert. And I kept tripping over the belt. Eventually, I felt badly about taking the guy's coat—he'd also left his Parkinson's meds in one of the pockets—so I returned it to the restaurant with an apologetic note about carrying it off by mistake. I didn't actually walk into the restaurant with the stolen jacket, of course—I just draped it across the giant bull's-head doorknobs around five o'clock in the morning. Now, I use a royal purple bathrobe that I got on sale at Sears. It makes me look like one of those mobsters who fake madness by wearing their pajamas on the subway. Pretty stylish. Not that it matters. If all goes according to plan, the last thing Mrs. Sproul will care about is my wardrobe.

I wait several yards from the entryway, under a shedding dogwood, pretending to smoke a cigarette. Soon enough, a mother nearly half my age appears with a double stroller. Not twins—just two kids about a year apart. The woman's got a plaster cast on one forearm, so she's appreciative when I offer to hoist the carriage wheels over the steps. I'm glad to be helpful. Then I slip inside behind her. Recent parents are always the key to entering any residential building. They have far more on their minds than collective security. If our own baby had worked out, I suppose I'd be the same way. Or if we could have another one. But it didn't. And we can't. So now my greatest concern is getting onto my former fifth grade teacher's fire escape without arousing suspicion. I loiter in the lobby until the young mother enters her apartment and then I climb to the second floor—with excessive determination, just in case I'm seen. The winding hallways are lined by ornate sconces, but only one bulb in each is functional. There's also a skylight on the second floor. A brass plaque beside the trash chute warns against tossing lit cigars into the compactor. From the flat opposite the utility closet comes the sound of afternoon sex. I breathe through my mouth to block out the pungent stench of grubby carpet and wet dog, trying several doors until I find the stair access to the roof.

Outside, the sun is a glowing patch of haze. Not much up here but a stack of folded aluminum chairs propped against a low parapet. Also empty Rolling Rock bottles, configured to form a giant question mark. Some have cigarette butts floating in them. I stand in the shadow of one of the tall brick chimneys and trade my street garb for the mask and robe. I'm able to alter my getup in fifty-five seconds. I've timed myself. But when I lower my body down the fire escape toward Mrs. Sproul's window, it feels as though I've been changing my clothes on the roof for an eternity.

Okay, timeout. You're probably wondering what an ordinary, straight-shooting, middleclass guy is doing showing his pecker to post-menopausal women up and down the Connecticut coast. A legitimate question. But I'm not sure how well I can answer it. If you'd told me a year ago, when my family room was loaded high with Hefty bags of hand-me-down toddler clothes, that I'd be systematically flashing senior citizens, I'd have laughed my ass off. Or socked you one. My temper's not my strong suit. But post-baby, now that the Minnie-Mouse tutus and Winnie-the-Pooh sweater-sets have been shipped off to Dawn's lesbian cousin, who's expecting in a matter of weeks, it seems entirely natural to play my ongoing game of show the salami. Somehow, it gives my daily existence as sense of wholeness, of direction. And there's a certain reassurance in knowing that, by taking on a small amount of personal risk, I can begin to even out the cosmic score.

We were at an early Christmas party down in Bondleigh Cove when the inspiration first came to me. It's an annual shindig hosted by the volunteer historian at Dawn's preservation society. Dr. Tugman's quite well-off—he's a retired orthodontist and used to live in a three-story Victorian up on Prospector's Hill—but after his wife fell off a ladder two summers ago, he relocated to one of those refurbished upscale complexes opposite the public beach. I mention all of this because his holiday party was right after Dawn lost the baby, and she didn't want to go out at all, but she has a soft spot for the old widower, compounded by mutual loss, and eventually I talked her into making a brief appearance. Just say hello and shake a few hands, I promised. One drink, tops. But as I'd hoped, she started chatting with the courtly old fellow, and with another woman whose father had designed some celebrated covered bridges in Vermont, and pretty soon Dawn was deep into her second glass of champagne.

I interrupted the conclave only to ask after the lavatory. I'd already poked my head into several rooms unsuccessfully—a broom cabinet, a linen closet, a pantry. Tugman chuckled. "You have to go *through* the pantry. It used to be the servant's bedroom," he explained. "And be sure to pull shut the shower curtain. I'm still without drapes in the second bathroom, I'm afraid, and there's no need to give the neighbors a thrill." The old dentist laughed, his crimson face aglow under his shock of white hair. "Of course, if you do want to give them a thrill, I suppose nobody will stop you." He turned back toward his audience, dabbing his forehead with a silk handkerchief. "That's the tradeoff. A priceless view of the Sound out front, but in back it's all kitchens and toilets." This last remark sent the man reeling into another bout of mirth.

I crossed the parlor, where an overweight foursome crowded around the piano, crooning "It's a Long Way to Tipperary," off-key, then passed through the pantry into the second bathroom. It was a tidy little chamber, adorned in faded vermillion. Above the wainscoting, the wallpaper depicted the silhouettes of wildflowers—probably a popular design in its era, but today one seemingly more suited for toilet tissue. Tiny archers were carved along the frame of the mirror. The clothes hamper had been built into the wall. Maybe, when they'd refurbished these apartments, they also hadn't been able to find the servants' quarters. I took a closer look at the bath area. Tugman wasn't lying: From the window, you could indeed see the interior of the apartment across the courtyard. At fifteen feet, you could even make out the subscripts on the television newscast. And the individual polka dots on the viewer's dressing gown. I was about to draw shut the nylon bath curtain—when I recognized the woman watching TV in the opposite flat. Ms. O. Cotz-Cupper! The same screwy bitch who'd raised all hell when I wouldn't fill her sister's prescription for Vicodin. I'd told her: The name on the prescription has to match the name on the ID. No exceptions. In reality, if it had been amoxicillin or Lipitor, I'd have bent the rules, but hydrocodone is high-powered stuff. The kind of stuff the government tracks. So I wouldn't do it. Period. Then she called company headquarters, and got hold of the New England field supervisor, who backed me up, one hundred percent, but that's still a note in my permanent file. Customer complaint. What a goddam bitch! And somehow, while I was taking care of my business in the bathroom, I already knew my next step.

A few minutes later, I slipped out of the party with a black towel under my shirt. Then it was up to the roof, over a concrete dividing wall, down the opposite fire escape. Just enough time in between to strip and wrap the towel around my lower face. When O. Cotz-Cupper turned toward the window, I knew I'd succeeded. Her hands clutched to her blouse, as though she were covering her own nakedness, and her mouth opened like she wanted to scream, but she was afraid to. I could sense already that she wouldn't report me. That for years to come, she'd lock windows while sleeping and peek nervously behind closed drapes. She'd carry around a perpetual, latent terror—like an aneurysm waiting to rupture. A far greater punishment than the assault she expected. That seems like a fair trade-off for the permanent notation in my consumer relations file.

So I climbed back up the fire escape, changed back into my party clothes, and returned to Dr. Tugman's flat. By the time Dawn was ready to depart, an hour later, I was at the piano, belting out "Auld Lang Syne."

~

And now I'm here on Mrs. Sproul's fire escape. She's gone over to the kitchen sink to wash some dishes, so she doesn't hear my tapping above the running water. I thump harder on the glass. Still no reaction. I have no choice but to stick my upper torso through the big open window, searching for something that will draw the old woman's notice. There's a stainless steel pot suspended from a nail in the molding. Perfect for banging against the iron radiator. That should do the trick—and it does. Now Mrs. Sproul turns to face me. I attempt to meet her gaze, but she's not looking at me. She's looking somewhere over my left shoulder. The old woman blinks normally, and the eyeballs shift back and forth, but the eyes themselves are unmistakably blank. Fucking brilliant! I'm flashing a goddam blind woman. It crosses my mind that I'll make her touch me—like the Braille version of flashing—but then something gives, and I lose my grip on the window sash, and suddenly I'm sprawled out across the linoleum.

"Who's that?" demands Mrs. Sproul.

I hold still and say nothing, as I might do if approaching a wild bird or rabbit.

"I know someone's there," she says. "Who are you and what do you want?"

Again, I keep silent. My head throbs. Blood is trickling down the side of my left ear, and it tickles. Immediately opposite me is a metal cabinet door with a calendar attached by magnets. The magnets read: "Have you taken your blood pressure medication today?" The calendar is turned to July, 1995. Beside the cupboard rests an olive-green wall telephone with a rotary dial. If the old woman goes for the phone, I know I'll be forced to restrain her. But she doesn't go for the phone. Instead, Mrs. Sproul pokes my flank with her open-toed slipper. Before I know it, she's leaning over my midsection and she's holding a carving knife in both hands. She's got it raised above her shoulder, like she's about to reenact the murder scene from a Roman tragedy. I can probably wrestle the weapon from her, but not without doing her physical damage. And that, of course, is across my moral line. "I may not see so well, but I'm not stupid," she says. "I can tell you're conscious by how you're breathing. Now account for yourself. Whoever you are. Speak up."

She doesn't sound frightened. Merely annoyed. As though confronting a wayward child. Of course, she can't see that my robe is hanging open. While I'm trying to decide my next move—whether I'll be able to crawl to the front door without getting stabbed—she's inching her bath slipper along my leg. Then—without warning—she drives her heel into my crotch. I groan, struggling for breath. When I try to sit up, I hit my head on the corner of the cupboard door.

"I warned you. Next time, it's the knife. Now, who are you?"

"Please, Mrs. Sproul," I say. "It's William Honegger. Billy. From the fifth grade."

She waves the knife aggressively, keeping it in constant motion—maybe to prevent me from lunging for it. "You don't sound like you're in fifth grade," she says.

"Not now," I say. "A long time ago. You taught me in the fifth grade."

"What was that name you said?"

"William Honegger. H-O-N-E-G-G-E-R"

The corners of her mouth tighten. She's thinking. "I remember William Honegger."

"You do?"

"Stupid boy," she says. "Dumb as a box of bricks."

I'm not sure how to respond to this. As absurd as it may sounds, her remark genuinely hurts me. Almost as badly as my testicles, which ache all the way into my shoulders.

"Funny that," adds Mrs. Sproul—more to herself than to me. "I always thought I'd remember the gifted ones. The future scientists, the scholars. The young ladies who'd turn heads entering a ballroom….But all I recall are the most deplorable of the lot—the ones who lacked any hope." She's still poised to impale me, the knife trembling in her grip. "Life's a funny business. You can tell some of them are hopeless from the outset—even at the age of ten, eleven, twelve—and yet you've got to go on pretending otherwise. That's the only way."

I wipe the blood from my neck with my sleeve. "I wasn't sure you'd remember me," I say.

"Honegger, Honegger," says Mrs. Sproul. "Of course, I remember: Dirty little runt. Had the makings of a pervert." She draws the knife back suddenly—as though to gain momentum. "You're not a pervert, are you?"

"I'm a pharmacist," I say.

"Hmmm. Could be." That's classic Wilma Sproul—never affirming anything. The same noncommittal "could be" she offered if you explained you hadn't done your homework because your grandmother had passed on. "Pharmacists aren't what they used to be, I suppose. In my day, pharmacy was a distinguished profession." Here, Mrs. Sproul begins coughing violently. Her temples pulse and the color drains from her long, downy jowls. She lowers the knife, straining for air.

I stand up. "Are you okay?"

"I'm fine. Stay back," she snaps. She removes a crumpled tissue from her blouse cuff, spits into it, then stuffs it back up her sleeve. "Now speak up. What are you doing here? I didn't phone for a pharmacist."

It's difficult to gauge her mental status. She sounds lucid, but there's something a bit hazy in her speech—though probably not enough to risk pretending that I've entered through the front door.

"I rang the bell," I say. "You didn't answer."

"I didn't?" she replies. "No, I suppose I didn't. That's what happens when you're nearing the end."

"You didn't answer the bell," I say. "So I thought I'd knock on the window."

This seems to appease her. "Very sensible." She shrugs. "William Honegger, a pharmacist. He was *such* a stupid boy."

I tear off a paper towel and run it under the cold water. The gash in my ear is far deeper than I anticipated. The cartilage protrudes through the skin.

"You have any antiseptic? I did a job on myself when I fell."

"Whatever I have is above the sink," she answers. She has already lowered the carving knife to her side, and now she deposits it on the countertop behind her. Then she reaches for it again quickly—as though the peculiarity of my appearance has finally broken through her blood-brain barrier—but the weapon is already tucked into the pocket of my robe. I can see the first twinge of fear on her face as she searches, running her brittle fingers over the Formica like a spider's legs. "What do you want with me, young man?" she demands. "My niece will be here any moment now."

So it's not a granddaughter. It crosses my mind that Mrs. Sproul may also be childless, like Dawn and me, and I feel sincerely sorry for her. For a moment or two. But there's a whole world of people who've got it rough—children battling cholera without tetracycline and that sort of thing—so you can't let it get to you.

"Doreen comes every week," says Mrs. Sproul. "She's fiercely devoted."

"Is she?" I ask. The cupboard above the sink contains a trove of germicides no longer recommended by the Food & Drug Administration. Hydrogen peroxide. Lugol's iodine. Mercurochrome. That leaves me with only two options: soap and water. "In that case," I say, "I'll just wash off my cut and get out of your way."

That's when the complexity of my predicament wallops me: I can't just walk out the door and put this behind me. She's bound to tell the niece that I've come crashing through her window—and one question will inevitably lead to another. When you've exposed yourself to fourteen women, you can't afford to be careless.

"I just wanted to say hello," I add. "I'm visiting *all* of my old teachers. On account of I'm turning forty next month."

"Forty and a pharmacist." The old lady coughs again—but not as roughly. "You haven't visited that nitwit Tillary, have you?"

"Not yet," I say. "You're my first."

This answer seems to please the old woman. "And why shouldn't I be?"

"You were my favorite." It costs me a lot to say this—but it's better than ten years in the slammer. That's the amazing thing about this country: You knife some guy in a bar, they give you a few months in jail. But you drop your pants in the wrong place, it's off to the federal pen and they throw away the key. "Not a day goes by when I don't think about a lesson I learned in the fifth grade."

"How very sweet," she says. "I'm pleased you didn't turn out as badly as we all thought. Surprised. Shocked. But pleased, never-the-less."

I don't have the ego to ask who "we all" are.

"That nitwit Tillary was the only one who thought you'd amount to anything other than a sex offender. But that was part of her idiocy. She thought *all of the children* were going to alter the course of western civilization for the better. Every one of you was an up-and-coming Michelangelo." Mrs. Sproul winced—at a thought as painful to her as angina. "It sounds all fine and dandy on paper. She's the angel. I'm the ogre. But if you believe all the children are up-and-coming Michelangelos, you can't teach them a darn thing. Do you see what I'm saying?"

"I guess so," I say.

"Don't guess," snaps Mrs. Sproul. "This isn't a game show."

While I'm dabbing my ear, Mrs. Sproul reaches her hand to my face and starts running her bony fingers over the features. At first, I fear she's going to poke my eyes out—her means of leveling the playing field. But she's just "looking" at me, in her way. Tapping the end of my nose. Measuring the width of my eyebrows. I feel like I'm being fitted for a balaclava under the care of a master tailor. Then she draws back. "Not a bad face," she says.

"Thank you."

"Not *handsome*, but it'll suffice."

"I hope so," I say, aware that the niece may stop by at any moment with the week's groceries—and I'm wearing only a robe. "I'm glad to see you're doing well, but I should probably be going now."

I start inching toward the foyer—just as Mrs. Sproul succumbs to another coughing fit. "My husband's smoking," she says, matter-of-fact. "Left me coughing and blind. Macular degeneration. Left Lawrence dead. At least, that's what they believe *this week*. So I am not, as you say, 'doing well.' But I'd be pleased if you would stay for a cup of tea. Keep me company until Doreen gets here."

I try to make excuses, but she ignores them and turns on the gas. "William Honegger," she says—again. As though repeating my name will somehow make it more palatable. "In spite of myself, I am pleased that you dropped in. It is very thoughtful. Not many of my little ladies and gentleman remember me anymore."

"They're probably just very busy," I say.

She sits down at the metal folding table. Reluctantly, I pull up a chair opposite her. The placemats depict capitals of Western Europe—London, Paris, Rome and Berlin. But in this frozen world, Berlin is still perpetually divided between East and West.

"Busy, my left foot. They probably just don't give a darn," says my hostess. "My fifth grade teacher was Miss Llywarch. Adara. That's Welsh for 'catcher of birds.' She was a beautiful woman—a girl really, probably not even twenty-five. When the war started, she returned to Britain and was killed in an air raid."

"I'm sorry."

"That's the only reason I know what happened to her. Because she was killed by the Nazis. Otherwise, she'd just have evaporated into the ether."

Mrs. Sproul looks as though she might weep, but she doesn't. The kettle whistles, a long mournful hum. When I try to help her pour the tea, she slaps away my hand. Hard enough to sting. I can only imagine what havoc she might have rendered with that carving knife. The old woman's hands shake fiercely while she fills our cups, but not a drop of the hot beverage lands outside the saucers. "Maybe I was too hard on Tillary," she says, apropos of nothing. "I suppose she meant well—in her way. When you do see her, please send my best." I pledge that I will. Then we sip hot tea in the stifling apartment while I struggle for something else to say. The old lady's eyes have acquired the filmy detachment of daydreams. I wonder if she is thinking about me, or her long lost students, or Adara Llywarch dying in the war.

"I should really be going," I announce. I'm ever conscious that the niece may be unloading groceries from her car as we speak.

Mrs. Sproul looks up from her cup. She appears surprised—as though she's forgotten about me. "Do you live around here?" she asks.

"Y—yes," I say, a bit hesitantly. But what harm can it do, right? She already knows my name. "I've got a place up in North Bondleigh. On Mill Creek."

"And you're a pharmacist?"

"That's what I said. At Metro Drugs."

"Could be," says Mrs. Sproul—in a way that makes me want to deck her. "Only drugstore around here used to be Rexall's. Back when pharmacists were legitimate professionals. Not foreigners who couldn't make it as doctors." Mrs. Sproul grins, as though this characterization brings her pleasure. She still has her own teeth, aligned in well-ordered rows. "Are you married, William Honegger?"

"Am I married?" I echo. Another straight-forward question—requiring only a one word response. But I don't give it. Instead, with a different word, I suddenly obliterate my fourteen years with Dawn. It's not unlike it was with Arnold/Sally. That's what we were going to call the baby. Arnold, after Dawn's late father, if it was a boy. Sally—just because we liked the sound of it—if it was a girl. But then we stopped calling it anything, and it stopped being anything. Just like that. So, for the moment, it's the same with my marriage. "No, I'm not married," I say. And I regret it instantly.

"Good," says Mrs. Sproul "Neither is my Doreen."

"I *really* should be going now," I say again. More forcefully. I'm about to add: I have plans to see my wife—but I realize this claim will no longer make any sense. "I need to get back to work," I lie.

"Stay a few more minutes. I would *so* like you to meet my niece," the blind woman says. "My Doreen is a bit feral. Like an alley cat. But she's a true dear. Quite frankly, a dullard pharmacist might do her some good."

"I wish I could, but—

"—Oh, that reminds me. There is something else I want to show you," she says, ignoring my protests. "In the foyer."

66

Mrs. Sproul pushes her chair away from the table and disappears through the kitchen door. I feel obliged to follow. Or maybe powerless to resist, like one of the Pied Piper's children. And, although I know rationally that Mrs. Sproul survives quite fine on her own, there's something wrong to me about abandoning an elderly blind woman. So it's out of the sweltering kitchen, into the broiling foyer.

The foyer is a low railroad car of a room with matching armoires on either side of the entryway. One contains commemorative dishes of the Franklin Mint variety. *Gone With the Wind.* "Washington Crossing the Delaware." The other holds an assortment of cheap European souvenirs and African decorative arts—from which a research anthropologist might piece together the retirement itineraries of "L. & W. Sproul." My hostess shuffles to the second cabinet and points toward the top. She's indicating a silver plaque in the shape of a globe.

"Would you read that? Aloud, please."

I take down the plaque and dust off its surface; the metal could use a thorough polishing. "Forty years of devoted service," I read. "A life dedicated to her 'young ladies' and 'young gentleman'."

Mrs. Sproul nods approvingly. "That's right. Forty years. I *earned* that plaque."

"Forty years *is* a long time," I say.

"Forty years is a long time," she answers. "So they gave me a plaque. And now I can't even read it."

That's when the door buzzer sounds. Like a dagger through the stagnant air.

"May I visit the young gentlemen's room?" I interject—somehow, in my desperation, I've reclaimed the language of fifth-grade subservience. But then I bolt across the apartment without waiting for the old woman's permission. I don't seek out the bathroom, of course, but the master bedroom. Or, to be more precise, the walk-in cedar closet. It's dusty and stinks caustically of nail polish remover. Also a faint hint of mildew. Fortunately, Lawrence Sproul's business suits remain entombed on the hangers along the far wall. Lots of gabardine and tweed. Sports coats with suede elbow patches, the pockets smelling of stale pipe tobacco. All very collegiate. I'm somewhat shorter than the dead man was, but I manage to hike my belt up to my navel and conceal its odd location under a cashmere sweater. At least, Sproul's penny-loafers fit well. And the shoulders of his Oxford shirts are just the right width. I examine myself in the rectangular mirror above the bureau. I do appear marginally presentable, if thirty years behind the times. Yeah, right. Who the hell am I fooling? I look like I mugged the grandfather on a 1950s sitcom.

And then genius strikes. I un-tuck the Oxford and tear a gash in one of the jacket sleeves. I retrieve a bright yellow necktie, vintage seventies, from a chair-back and drape it loose around my neck. Noose-like. As though I'm impersonating a suicidal clown. From a wall peg, I retrieve a gray peddler's cap—and I set it atop my skull, jauntily askew. Now that's much better. I actually look trendy.

Or, at least *plausibly* trendy. Enough to snow Doreen. The niece is wearing an enormous denim skirt that looks more like a picnic umbrella. Or something Scarlett O'Hara might have worn during her Woodstock phase. The skirt has bells along the seams, and they jingle while she walks. Her top is low-cut latex. Dressed like that, she's certainly got no grounds to criticize.

Doreen looks up from the groceries when I enter the kitchen. A polite smile, then she looks away. Indifferent? Shy? Something more? The girl obviously does not remember my helping her with last week's bags.

"Hi," I say, trying to sound nonchalant. "I'm Bill Honegger."

~

The defining feature of Mrs. Sproul's fifth-grade classroom was its spareness. What a contrast to fourth grade, where Miss Mandlebaum posted construction paper cutouts with each changing season: Valentine's hearts for February, Irish shamrocks for March, umbrellas and Easter bunnies for April. Or even Dr. Duggan, in sixth grade, who kept the same Monet water lily prints on the walls, decade after decade. But unlike the other classrooms at Orestes Bronson Elementary, which looked so forlorn during the summers, when you peered through the plate-glass at the boxed decorations stockpiled like military rations beneath the chalkboards, Mrs. Sproul's room looked more or less the same year round. As austere in October as in July. Only the chairs stacked atop the desks gave away the month. That, and that the floor-to-ceiling window shades stood open through the long summer holiday. During the school year, when Mrs.

Sproul ordered the slats shut tightly, you had no way of watching the janitors lowering the flag before a storm, or of relishing the first dusting of snow on winter morning. Every school day, through the fluorescent dimness, Mrs. Sproul paced between the desks with her long wooden pointer. "Busy hands are happy hands," she warned us. "An idle mind is the devil's workshop." And we copied phrases like these, in Denelian script, until our little elbows ached.

My nemesis in fifth grade was a guy named Chuck Ziegler. He was one of Mrs. Sproul's "future scholars"—a fair-skinned kid with enormous blue eyes and an unequalled knowledge of reptiles and amphibians. At least among the ten year olds of coastal Connecticut. Chuck's father owned the local "Pet Paradise" and, at an age when access to snakes was more coveted than access to royalty, Chuck had parties where the popular boys could drape the boa constrictors over their shoulders. He was also the only student ever to earn a perfect mark on Mrs. Sproul's diagnostic spelling examination, after which he could commit no sin in her eyes. (In contrast, I scored something like seven out of one hundred.) But Chuck Ziegler, for reasons still beyond my understanding, devoted his towering fifth grade intellect to one principal crusade: My ongoing and perpetual humiliation. I suppose I was an easy target: short, pudgy, in the lowest groups in math and reading. Not the kind of child to generate great sympathy among his classmates or teachers. So nobody but me minded when Chuck Ziegler sneaked under my desk and tied my shoelaces together. Or when he filled my lunch box with liquid paper. Or when he scrawled large black swastikas on my desk and told Miss Tillary that I'd drawn them. But the worst came one recess in the winter, on the box-ball court, when Chuck offered to shake my hand to seal a truce. With his other hand, he shoved a tree frog down my dungarees.

You don't know discomfort until you've had a live frog in your trousers. The damn animal must have panicked, because it started squirming around my groin. I also panicked and tried to retrieve it with my fingers. But getting a live frog out of your pants is far harder than getting one in. And I was terrified it might bite the end off my penis. We'd just learned about eunuchs in our lesson on Ancient Egypt, and I wasn't taking any chances. So I did the only thing I could do: I unzipped my fly and poked my pecker through, to protect it while I hunted for the frog. That's when

Chuck Ziegler returned to the box-ball court with Mrs. Sproul in tow.

"My dear young man," she said. "This will not be tolerated."

I still had one hand protecting my exposed pecker and the other deep in my jeans. "He did this," I shouted. "He stuck a live frog in my pants."

"Could be," said Mrs. Sproul wearily. "Charles, did you put a frog in William's trousers?"

"No, ma'am," said Chuck Ziegler.

"I thought not," said Mrs. Sproul.

"You've got to believe me," I pleaded. "There's a fucking frog in my pants. I'll take them off and show you."

Mrs. Sproul shook her head in dismay. "What language! You'll do no such thing," she said. She pointed at my exposed member. "Take care of that right this instant. Unless you want me to hit it with a yardstick."

I zipped up my fly. I could still feel the frog, struggling against my thigh.

"You'll come with me now," said Mrs. Sproul. "You'll keep your hands on top of your head and you'll come with me."

"But the frog—"

"On top of your head," she insisted. I complied. She paraded me past my classmates like a prisoner of war.

"You'll spend your recreation time with me," she announced. "Until you learn to use it responsibly. Now be seated. And place your hands on the desktop, palms up."

I attempted several times that morning to show her the frog—which soon suffocated under the weight of my leg—but she refused to listen. Her only goal was to keep my hands away from my privates. And then I was compelled to repeat this exercise every morning for the entire remainder of the school year. I sat beside Mrs. Sproul, indoors, while all of the other students enjoyed the spring sunshine. If my hands left the desktop, even to scratch my nose, she snapped her ruler across the artificial wood. But I dared not complain, certainly not to my parents, because then they would learn the alleged cause of my punishment. Even Chuck Ziegler wasn't prepared for this extreme a sentence. He began avoiding me. I'd become his badge of dishonor. But he never confessed to shoving the frog down my pants. Meanwhile, Mrs. Sproul's glare immobilized my hands as effectively as five sets of Mexican finger traps.

"You'll be grateful someday, William," she said. Every recess. "The day will arrive when you'll thank me for molding you into a young gentleman."

"Thank you," I say. "But it's really not worth the trouble."

Doreen has offered to prepare a poultice for my ear. Some concoction involving bran flakes, aloe leaves and puréed tomatoes. "No trouble at all," she says, squeezing vegetables into the electric blender. "I'm the one who should be thanking you. Aunt Wilma doesn't get very many visitors." When the girl leans over the blender, driving the vegetables into the blades, her breasts nearly tumble out of her top.

"She was an excellent teacher," I say.

"Do you truly think that?" asks Mrs. Sproul. "Well, I think so too."

Doreen squeezes her aunt's hand. The girl's other hand is pink with tomato paste. "Of course, you were a wonderful teacher," she says—but in the manner that one speaks to elderly people about subjects that no longer matter. "Did you show Mr. Honegger your plaque?"

"—Bill," I say. "Please."

The girl smiles. She pours the contents of the blender onto a dishrag and drapes the cloth across my wound with a self-confidence that surprises me.

"Doreen is studying medicine," says Mrs. Sproul.

"Oh," I say.

"Holistic medicine," explains Doreen. "Herbal remedies."

"*Medicine*," Mrs. Sproul says again. More decisively. Then she adds: "Mr. Honegger's not married."

"Auntie!" The girl rolls her eyes—obviously for me, not for her aunt. "You're really in top form today, aren't you?"

"I'm just saying," says the blind woman.

"What are you saying, exactly?" asks the girl.

Her aunt sips from her second cup of tea. "Make hay while the sun shines," she says.

That's an expression I'll never forget. Probably copied it five thousand times. "Make hay while the sun shines." "Waste not, want not." "Can't never could do anything." An entire year of my life practicing penmanship on platitudes while Miss Tillary's class built the Great Pyramid out of papier-mâché. And after all that, my handwriting is still virtually illegible.

"Mr. Honegger is a pharmacist," says the blind lady. "*A pharmacist.*"

"That's right," I say. "I'm a pharmacist." But I wink at Doreen while

I say this—trying to hint that my drug trade may be broader than her aunt suspects.

"If you want my opinion, dear, pharmacy is a very distinguished profession," says Mrs. Sproul "He's practically a doctor."

"Practically," I say.

The niece has the poultice pressed to the side of my head. A cool lotion surrounded by her warm, gentle fingers. Impulsively, I raise my hand to my ear and place my own hand over hers.

"I'm sorry you fell," she says—as though our skin is not in contact. The girl lowers her voice to nearly a whisper. "It does her good to have people here. I hope you're not disappointed."

"Why should he be disappointed?" shouts Mrs. Sproul.

"He shouldn't be," says the niece.

"I'm not," I say.

We exchange a look of conspiracy.

"I was an excellent teacher," says Mrs. Sproul. "No matter what anybody says. I was a darn fine teacher. Darn fine." She breaks off to cough violently into her tissue. "I wouldn't do it any differently. Any of it."

Doreen's delicate hand is still pressed under mine. I'm afraid to move—afraid she'll pull away. How many years since I've done this—touched another human being with the outcome so uncertain? Not since meeting Dawn.

"Let them say what they will," says Mrs. Sproul. One large vein throbs behind her right eyebrow, but the rest of her face is suddenly lifeless. For the first time all afternoon, she looks as though the end really is near. Not just old, but too old. "We were teaching children—not competing for ribbons at a state fair. Or preening ourselves like debutantes at a ball. What did that sow Tillary know? Or any of them?! All that mumbo-jumbo about what the children wanted. *What the children wanted*! They were *children*, for heaven's sake. How could they possibly know what they wanted? I didn't even know what *I* wanted."

"It's all right," says Doreen.

"It is not all right," snaps her aunt. "It most certainly is not."

The girl's hand slides out from under mine. When the old woman starts sobbing, her niece is already at her side. "There, there," she soothes. "Would you like more tea?"

Mrs. Sproul shakes her head. She blows her nose with the force of a locomotive. "Forty years, and they wanted me to start over *their way*," she says. "With construction paper and papier-mâché! But I let them know what was what: If my methods were good enough for the likes of Adara Llywarch, then they were certainly good enough for me." Then the old woman turns to me and adds: "Miss Llywarch was my fifth grade teacher. A brilliant woman. She was killed in an air raid during the war."

"I'm very sorry," I say.

"They don't make schoolteachers like that anymore," answers Mrs. Sproul. "Tillary wasn't fit to wash that woman's boots."

"It was their loss," says Doreen. "They didn't know what they had."

Now her aunt says nothing. Not even: "Could be." She just sits impassively, her arms folded across her chest. I stand up. I know the time has come for my departure.

"I hope my visit hasn't upset you too much," I say.

The girl shakes her head. "Not at all. If you want to come back again, I'm sure Aunt Wilma would be happy to see you. Wouldn't you, Aunt Wilma?"

I try to read a deeper meaning into this question—a hint that the niece would also like me to return. It's hard to tell.

"Would you like Mr. Honegger to visit again?" asks the girl. Louder.

"Forty years," says the old blind woman. "My entire life."

"She would like it," says the niece. "Please do come."

"I'll certainly try," I say.

Of course, I know that I won't. And I can tell that Doreen knows this too. She accompanies me to the front door, and we exchange a quick handshake at the threshold. Then I climb back up to the roof and retrieve my clothing. My robe is still in Mrs. Sproul's bathroom, I realize. But that's fine. I doubt I'll be needing it anymore. Maybe the old widow will find some use for it. That seems like a fair trade, cosmically speaking, a stylish purple robe for the two marble lions that I now haul from the rear parking lot into the back of the Plymouth. I can already sense how much Dawn is going to like them. Once I've loaded them into the vehicle, side by side, I strap them into place with the seatbelts. Just as I might secure carpooling children. I enjoy looking at the marble lions through the rear-view mirror—forsaken animals on their way to a second life. A better life. Yes, a better life. We've just started on our journey home, and I can already feel their healing powers taking hold.

The Magic Laundry

When his father offered to stake him in any business venture of his choosing, Jeff Cutter decided to open a laundromat on the corner of Broadway and 117th Street in upper Manhattan. The old man was, of course, disappointed. He'd made his own fortune in a series of manufacturing enterprises as drab as they were lucrative—industrial adhesives, orthotic shoe insoles, articulating paper for dentists—and from his only son he had hoped for something a bit more glamorous. *Why not software design? Maybe robotics?* But after four years at Columbia University studying Demosthenes and Cicero, Jeff recognized his own limitations. He was an affable sort, neither inarticulate nor unhandsome, but too sincere to sell things and not shrewd enough to buy them. If among the classics under-grads at Columbia, he'd been considered rather a lightweight, he none-the-less preferred reading the Ancients (or a pick-up softball game, for that matter) to anything smacking of hard work and profit. A corner laun-dromat was about all he had in him. The elder Cutter asked: *How about a professional laundering service?* Or at least a dry cleaner's? But Jeff eventually won his father over with forecasts of a national chain of coin-operated laundromats that would do to full-service cleaners what Block-buster had done to drive-in movies. The name proved the decisive selling point: The Magic Laundry. Jeff's father thought it sounded Chinese—a killer advantage when it came to cleaning clothes.

Jeff spent his summer scouting out the neighborhood's three existing laundries. The largest, Kwick Wash Inc., catered primarily to the college crowd. While making use of fifty-one front load washers and three dozen mega dryers, patrons could play arcade games and foosball in a dimly lit alcove or watch ESPN on a large-screen television. The owner, an over-weight, chain-smoking Greek in his sixties, whose very presence seemed carcinogenic, turned a blind eye to paying customers who walked around with lit joints or gave blowjobs in the restrooms. Only two blocks away, serving a tamer crowd of predominantly black and Dominican women, a young Filipino couple named Segovia operated the Praise The Lord Laundry. Mrs. Segovia's sister-in-law was running for a city council nomination in the Democratic primary. The laundry doubled as her campaign headquarters. Two long fiberglass folding tables in back had been cleared of religious icons and plastic flowers to make room for a stack of placards reading "Santos for Harlem," and several mornings every week the Santos-Segovia faction of the local party held court around the detergent vending machine. One full afternoon in the Kwick Wash and another at Praise the Lord—drying the same load of clothing several dozen times in an effort to avoid appearing suspicious—convinced Jeff that neither establishment was the proper model for The Magic Laundry.

Madame Ursula's held more promise. A family of Polish immigrants ran the business, all women, all daughters and nieces of the proprietor. The eldest niece was a senior at Columbia whom Jeff had seen sporadically around campus; the youngest daughters, gangly twins, couldn't have been more than twelve. Madame Ursula was herself about fifty. She'd kept her figure and her long curveless hair remained the color of wild yellow irises. While none of her individual features displayed a singular beauty—her lips were a tad thin, her nose boasted a faint hook—they meshed into almost symphonic perfection. Rumor had it that she'd been a sex-worker in Amsterdam after the Berlin Wall fell, also that she'd once counted Gomulka and General Jaruzelski among her lovers. Jeff had no way of knowing. But as an upperclassman, he had freely joined the speculation regarding Madame Ursula's background, itself a time-honored tradition among her clientele of graduate students and starter couples, for whom the owner's mysterious origins were as much of a draw as the laundry's cozy orange lamps and rosewood folding tables. Jeff had always admired Madame Ursula's élan. During his summer of spying, he also grew to appreciate her talents as a businesswoman. She doled out carefully chosen kindnesses: If a stranger off the street requested change for parking, she would offer to have one of her daughters feed his meter later in the afternoon. She made it her business to know as much about her customers' lives as they did not know of hers—but she was discreet, savvy, omniscient yet never intrusive. Jeff had washed the same bag of towels fifty times over three weeks before he uncovered her secret: Madame Ursula never touched the cleaning equipment.

The niece, he realized, ran the show. She emptied the coin canisters, programmed the water temperatures, changed the lint filters. While her aunt presided over the salon—cautious never to appear a mere laundress— the niece kept silent watch from her perch atop the antique safe that served as a makeshift counter. The girl's name was Katrin. When she wasn't clearing sheets of fabric softener from dryer drums or unclogging exhaust ducts, she sat with her long pale legs dangling from the safe and read inconspicuously. One morning, Jeff noticed that she was reading Thucydides. She must be knocking off her Western Civilization requirement over the summer, he thought. Yet three days later, while the girl stood on the sidewalk haggling with a child labor inspector sent by the state, Jeff passed by the safe and noticed that the volume was in the original Greek. He considered striking up a conversation: one classicist to another. But the bell above the door jangled unexpectedly and the girl was suddenly approaching—and Jeff realized that she thought he was spying *on her*, rather than on the laundry, because what other than romance would drive a sane person to wash the same red towels over again and again, morning after morning, until they'd faded to a pinkish gray? Katrin smiled at him. Jeff quickly plucked his towels from the dryer, nearly scalding his hands in the process. He didn't stop walking until he reached the bodega on the corner.

Six weeks later—on the Tuesday after Labor Day—The Magic Laundry celebrated its grand opening. Three dozen triple-load washers. Forty-two 30-pound dryers. Walls plastered with movie posters from the thirties and forties. Jeff's father had suggested naming each machine after a Hollywood celebrity of the Golden Age, the way upscale delis often did with sandwiches, so little brass labels on the equipment paid tribute to the likes of Myrna Loy and Errol Flynn. The elder Cutter, fresh up from Florida and armed with the statistic that the majority of new laundromats fail within six months, also insisted upon an opening-day gimmick to crack the market. They offered free laundry from six am to midnight— served up with complementary daiquiris and piña coladas. *That* attracted a crowd: college freshmen, winos, a homeless woman who stripped to her underwear. Two plainclothes cops shut the party down around dusk and issued Jeff a summons for serving alcoholic beverages without a liquor license. After that, Jeff's business dwindled. He picked up a handful of regular customers, transfer students and families new to the neighborhood. He also acquired several unfortunates who had been banned from Praise the Lord and Madame Ursula's for repeated misdemeanors—stealing women's clothing, sexually harassing customers—or, as in the case of Mrs. Garcia, had willingly exiled themselves after verbal altercations with the management. But these patrons numbered in the teens, at most, and no quantity of glossy photographs from *The Grapes of Wrath* and *Double Indemnity* could compensate for Jeff's principal difficulty: Would-be customers avoided an empty laundry the way diners avoided under-trafficked restaurants.

In desperation, Jeff considered hiring local high school kids to pretend that they were paying patrons in an attempt to break this self-defeating cycle. Then two miracles occurred on successive afternoons: On Friday, Madame Ursula invited him to dine with her. On Saturday, Mrs. Garcia announced that Mae West—a.k.a. washer number sixteen—had cured her chronic incontinence.

~

Madame Ursula's eldest daughter delivered the invitation: a note handwritten on monogrammed stationery. At first, Jeff feared it might be some sort of condolence card—that the omniscient laundress would know of a death in his family before he did himself. But the discovery of a summons to "a most informal supper" shocked him nearly as much. Jeff looked up from the letter to find the daughter, a lanky teenager with a hint of copper in her hair, waiting like a nineteenth century valet. What did she want? A tip? He reached into his wallet and removed two crisp singles. The girl laughed and shook her head. "Are you coming?" she asked. He could hear her Dutch upbringing in her vowels. "Mama needs to know how many places to set." Jeff paused in confusion, then nodded. He had not considered the possibility, not even for a moment, that one might turn down an audience with Madame Ursula.

That evening Jeff rang the Luczaks' buzzer at precisely eight o'clock. The women lived on the top floor of a six story walk-up several doors down from their business. On the way there, he noticed that the eldest daughter sat perched atop the safe. That meant the niece—the girl who suspected him of stalking—would be at dinner. But what of it? He'd done nothing wrong. Yet as he climbed the uneven wooden staircase that led to Madame Ursula's threshold, his ears burned red with shame.

His hostess greeted him at the door. She was wearing a white summer skirt with blue trim and a matching navy top. "So good of you," she said. "So very good."

Jeff offered her his bouquet. One of the twins carried it away and returned with the flowers arranged in a vase.

"I have never believed in making food to wait," said Madame Ursula. "Over dinner, we'll chat."

She led him through a cluttered parlor. The room contained far too much furniture: mahogany highboys and dropfront secretaries and savonarola chairs upholstered with purple velvet. In one corner, a plastic cover formed the outline of a harp; in another, an antique gramophone rested atop a baby grand piano. A swinging door led into an equally over-furnished dining room where the table had been set for ten. Eight of the places were already occupied by the Luczak girls. Madame Ursula seated herself at the head of the table. By default, Jeff sat between the twins at the foot. "My Rosa has already dined," said Madame Ursula. "I hope you do not find yourself too much in confinement. It is so truly a to-do to place the leaves in the table."

"It's okay," said Jeff. "I'm used to chow mein and pizza."

Madame Ursula motioned for one of the girls to begin the dinner service. "Well I fear I have no chow mein and pizza for you, Mr. Jeff Cutter. Tonight, we shall have escargot and Pemequid oysters. Oysters are to your liking, no?"

"Of course," lied Jeff. He'd never before tasted a Pemequid oyster. His primary goal was to avoid eye contact with the niece.

"I'm glad to see that you're an oyster connoisseur, Mr. Jeff Cutter," continued Madame Ursula. "Too few young men these days take such an interest. I am partial to Malpeques myself, but they have too much salt for Katrin's palate. Her tongue prefers a more fruitful oyster like the Pine Island, or an almond flavor like, I need not say, the Pemequid."

Jeff preferred not to think about Katrin's tongue. He waited nervously for his hostess to reveal the cause for his summons, but through dinner she spoke only of shellfish, of Turganev novels, of an article she'd read on the poaching of tigers. The word laundry never crossed her lips. Meanwhile, the younger girls whispered among themselves and giggled in periodic waves. Jeff felt as though he were caught in a summer-stock production of *Little Women*. He had read several stories in which unsuspecting young men like himself had been invited to such gatherings in the hope of arranging a marriage, and he began to worry about which of the underage girls his hostess had designated his. To his surprise, Madame Ursula concluded an anecdote about the cousin who supplied her with the free oysters, and she rose from the table. "Ladies," she said. The younger girls, as though trained, filed out of the room.

"It was a joy, Mr. Jeff Cutter," said Madame Ursula. "Now 'poof!' and I'm gone."

Suddenly, Jeff found himself alone with the niece. All that separated them was a graveyard of greasy dishes and balled-up napkins and empty oyster shells.

Katrin grinned. "You remind me of Elpenor."

"Of course," Jeff played along. "I do." He could think of no acquaintance with that name—if Elpenor were, in fact, a person.

"You don't have a clue," said Katrin. Her accent was thicker than her cousin's, but her voice flowed much more gently.

"Sure, Elpenor," ventured Jeff. "Hamlet's hometown."

"Elpenor," answered Katrin. "From the Odyssey, Book X. Odysseus' friend who drinks too much and falls off Circe's roof. You remind me of him."

"Okay," said Jeff. He refilled his water glass from the pitcher.

"We know nothing about him, of course," explained Katrin. "He was just some random guy who fell off a roof and was immortalized forever. But I imagine if we did know what he was like, he'd be something like you."

"Maybe," said Jeff. "I don't drink."

"We know," said Katrin. "If you did, we wouldn't hire you."

"What?"

The girl stood up and began to gather the dishes. "Don't look so surprised," she said. "My aunt wants to hire you to manage her business. I can't do it full time—not if I'm going to go to grad school next year."

Katrin rounded the table; she stood beside Jeff. The bare expanse of white flesh just below her collarbone breathed in and out only inches from his face. "I have a business myself, you know," said Jeff. When he realized that their conversation was to be professional in nature, he quickly grew disappointed and irritable.

"Get real, Jeff," said Katrin. "You won't last six months."

Jeff looked away from her chest. "I'm doing fine."

"You're not even making overhead," she answered. "The neighborhood can't support a fourth laundry. If you bail out now, your father can write off the machines." Katrin carried a stack of plates into the kitchen. "It's a good deal, Elpenor," she added when she returned. "Take it."

Jeff didn't answer.

"It's not magic, you know. I watch. I listen. I find out about people. I know your father fronted you the money in cash even though he wanted you to build rockets or something."

"Robots," said Jeff.

"Robots," agreed Katrin, speaking quickly. "And I know that you're single."

Katrin appeared surprised by her own audacity. She blushed, but didn't look away. They heard a car alarm raving at some distance.

"If we're done talking business," Katrin said softly, "you could invite me to dinner next weekend."

"You're serious," said Jeff. "You really mean it." His previous interactions with women had always been slow and uncertain. "Give me a minute. This doesn't happen very often."

Katrin smiled. "Elpenor only fell off the roof once."

They made arrangements to go out the following Saturday. Jeff felt grateful, also confused. She walked him to the door and he turned to face her at the threshold—even though he knew they would not kiss. "I have a question," he said. "What did your aunt do back in Poland?"

"You won't tell anyone?"

"Not a soul."

Katrin squeezed his arm. "We lived in Krakow," the girl said. "My aunt was the assistant supervisor of a public laundry."

The following day began with a bloodbath. A disturbed twelve year-old-boy from the General Grant housing projects had pilfered another child's puppy and tossed it unnoticed into one of the running washers. At the moment, Bonnie Williams had been changing her grandson's diaper in the restroom. She returned to find globs of knotted hair and a bloated cocker spaniel tangled in her brassieres and garters. Jeff offered her $1,000 in cash and free laundry for life to keep the matter quiet. What else could he do? Let her report it? Tell her to take the matter up with a prepubescent derelict? He paid another $500 in hush money to the mother of the puppy's owner. He even agreed to bury the drowned animal in a memorial garden for departed pets. Yet scouring the washer—a fifty pounder named Gregory Peck—Jeff felt only relief: Thank God it hadn't been a child.

Saturday afternoon was usually a period of peak demand, but a bout of Indian Summer kept traffic light. Mrs. Garcia came in around four. With her were two other squat companions in their sixties, possibly sisters; they shared close-cropped gray hair and broad ski-slope noses that reminded Jeff of snow shovels. He paid the three women little heed, at first. Mrs. Garcia knew only two topics for conversation: her husband's hypochondria and her own legitimate illnesses. She had initially come to The Magic Laundry in the most unlikely manner. In September, her husband had experienced acute chest pains while dropping her off at the Praise the Lord. The Filipino couple had insisted upon summoning a doctor. A shouting match ensued. When the physician, an anesthesiologist who happened to be Segovia's half-brother, diagnosed the pains as acid reflux, Mrs. Garcia declared herself vindicated and shifted her loyalties to Jeff. He thought her a dour, embarrassing woman. Yet that afternoon—and the novelty caught his attention—she was smiling like the Buddha.

Jeff stopped scrubbing and listened.

"This one right here, Henny" said Mrs. Garcia. "I'm sure of it. I always use Mae West for mine and the Keystone Cops one for Al."

The sister named Henny laughed shrilly. "The Keystone Cops are some riot."

"Not to live with."

Mrs. Garcia wiggled her rump. "No more leaking. No more wicking for me. I feel like one of those Depend commercials." She beckoned Jeff with two fingers. "You got a regular goldmine here, you know that," she said.

Jeff approached nervously. He'd wrapped his sleeves around his elbows, but they'd managed to get soaked anyway. "Is everything okay, ma'am?"

"Better than okay. Hunky-dory. Mae West here fixed my bladder."

"Your bladder?"

"I washed my overpants here last week and I've had complete control ever since. How common is this?"

"I'm not sure."

"Well you got to advertise better," said Mrs. Garcia. "Let people know what you're doing here."

Jeff took a step backwards. "I guess," he said.

"I tell you what," said Mrs. Garcia. "You done me a favor. I'll do you a favor. Half the people I know wet their beds. You'll have them taking numbers."

Jeff assured Mrs. Garcia that her assistance wasn't necessary—that he would prefer not to have it, in fact—but direct confrontation was not his strong suit. When he opened the laundry at six a.m. the following morning, two other women were standing in front of the iron guard gate carrying hampers. Every hour brought additional inquiries for the miracle-working machine—which was also rumored to treat herpes and lumbago. Potential customers called for reservations. Some walk-ins despaired of ever accessing Mae West—she was already booked five days in advance—and took their chances with less illustrious washers. Yet when the superintendent of a building on 126th Street announced that Gary Cooper, machine number eight, had substantially reduced his impotence, the entire establishment acquired a palliative halo. Later, a further discovery: Washing the discarded clothes of friends or relatives—even if they did not wear them again—might have transformative effects. Jeff started a mail-order business. He raised rates to two dollars per load. On Wednesday, he grossed twice as much as he had done in all of September.

Nobody ever credited The Magic Laundry with any earth-shattering miracles of the cancer-curing, world peace variety. It appeared that Jeff's machines, like their owner, recognized their limits. Yet each morning brought word of hemorrhoids soothed and passions reignited and reconciliations with long estranged siblings. Different washers gained reputations for aiding with specific problems. Humphrey Bogart, number three, helped smokers quit. Ronald Reagan, number twenty-eight, blocked out bad memories. Monetary difficulties were the province of number nine, Orson Welles. Bonnie Williams won $248 dollars on a scratch-and-match ticket and pinned a thank you card on the iron guard gate. A Carmelite nun experienced a particularly vivid dream about the Virgin Mary; she promised to praise The Magic Laundry in her prayers. Jeff's meteoric rise soon drew media attention. A chirpy female reporter netted an exclusive interview with Mrs. Garcia and photographed her kissing Jeff's cheek in front of Mae West. The headline on Friday's *New York Post* read: Machine Dry. Jeff's father even flew up from Cormorant Island to congratulate him on his "business acumen"; he insisted that they each smoke a Cuban cigar. "If you've got it, you've got it," the elder Cutter told the *Post.* "And my boy—make sure you quote me on this now—he's got it."

The reporter turned to Jeff. "Do you really think your machines perform miracles, Mr. Cutter? Increase fertility and improve test scores?"

"I'll answer that," interjected Jeff's father. "Our washers here at The Magic Laundry help those who are willing to help themselves."

"What exactly do you mean?" persisted the reporter.

The elder Cutter elaborated. "We do our part. The customers do theirs."

Jeff's part, it turned out, was too much for one man. When business had been sluggish, he did not think twice about leaving the store unmanned. With thousands of dollars in the till at any given moment, he could no longer afford such a luxury. He hired four employees in two days: three college students to cover the overnight and a gay black man known as Doc Happy to back him up during the day. Doc Happy was seventy-two and played the harmonica professionally in the evenings. Jeff had hoped that the old man's presence would give him more time to read—at least to review the Homeric passage about Elpenor before his date—but training an employee was a job in itself. When Saturday evening rolled around, Jeff still hadn't cracked a book.

High on confidence—although worn to the bone—Jeff prepared for his dinner with Katrin. Deep down, he doubted the powers of the miracle washers. Still, he cleaned his slacks and sweater in a machine reputed to foster romance. Clark Gable, number one. If you've got it, he assured himself, I guess you've got it.

Jeff picked Katrin up at Madame Ursula's. It was his first New York City date. He'd had a serious girlfriend back in Florida through his junior year, but she'd fallen for a German scuba instructor while on vacation in Honduras. Jeff's mother sent him their wedding announcement from the *Cormorant Island Sentinel*. When the couple went diving in Indonesia on their honeymoon and the groom died of an asthmatic attack, Jeff's mother sent him the obituary as well. After that, Jeff kept a low romantic profile. All of the women he'd met in New York were a little too something—though exactly what, he couldn't say—and he feared they might interpret his advances as insults. He'd expected to find Katrin sitting atop the antique safe in jeans and a t-shirt. Her low-cut black dress and high-heel shoes caught him off guard. The girl was exchanging whispers with her copper-haired cousin when Jeff peered through the window. She glided out to meet him, waving at the cousin and flashing him a puckish smile.

"Where to, Elpenor?"

"Oh, Jesus," said Jeff. "I don't know."

Katrin laughed. "Most girls would be really angry at you just about now. You know that, don't you?"

Jeff liked that she wasn't mad. "But you're not most girls," he said.

"We'll have Senegalese," she said. "Don't forget your wallet."

Katrin led him to a cozy, informal West African eatery on the ungentrified slope of Morningside Park. The tables were long, cafeteria-style. They sported checkered plastic coverings—some white and red, others white and green. The carcass of a mutilated payphone hung from one of the rear walls. Katrin embraced the maitre d'—a stylish dark-skinned woman in tight clothes—and she and Jeff took at seat beside the fish tanks. They were the only two white faces in the place.

"You should order the theibou djeb and aloko," suggested Katrin. "Snapper with plantains. And you should deep-six this miracle washer nonsense."

Jeff couldn't focus on Katrin and choosing his meal at the same time. He dropped the menu helplessly on the table. "Why on earth would I do that?"

"Because it's not you," she said. "Because it will consume every last waking minute of your time and you won't play softball again all fall."

"I hired four people today. Now *I* have a manager."

Katrin's cheeks flushed. "Bully for you, Elpenor," she said. "Has it crossed your mind that what you're doing is wrong? That you're taking advantage of those people?

"Of Mrs. Garcia? She's happy as a freshly-diapered baby."

The waitress came for their order. Jeff pointed to the theibou djeb and aloko. Yet when she asked if he preferred the aloko with peppers or with tamarind sauce, Katrin came to his rescue. She still had the upper hand after the waitress left.

"How about wrong to the Segovias or Timon Demopolis? How about wrong to my aunt?" Katrin's breath quickened. Her breasts rose and fell. "She can't afford many more weeks like this one. Do you know how hard my aunt works to keep her business going?"

Jeff pounced. "You mean how hard *you* work. I watch things, too."

"Yes, dammit, how hard *I* work," Katrin shot back. "I'm going to go to grad school next year and I'm going to teach classics and...." She stopped suddenly. "Look, I'm sorry."

"Tell me more about Elpenor," he said.

And she did. Their intimacy was instantaneous and almost brutal. They talked about the unspeakable—about her uncle's death in an electrical fire, how her father had killed her mother and then himself. They discussed under what circumstances it would be moral to assassinate the president. She admitted that she'd made out with a middle-aged woman in the ladies' room at the Kwick Wash. When the restaurant closed, they continued their conversation out onto the sidewalk and up to the steps of his building. It was nearly two-thirty. Several gypsy cabs slowed down to see if they wanted a lift; otherwise, the streets were deserted. Jeff didn't want to detain Katrin beyond reasonable first date hours, but he didn't want the conversation to end.

"Usually the *guy* walks the *girl* home, Elpenor," said Katrin. Her face flashed red in the light from the twenty-four hour pharmacy.

Jeff didn't know what to say. "That's a beautiful dress," he said.

"You can keep it," answered Katrin. "I'll leave it here."

She took him by the hand and led him up the stairs to his own apartment. They stood face to face at the door. "I'll give you the dress now," she said. "You'll give me sweats and a t-shirt in the morning."

"Are you sure you want to do this?" he asked.

"I don't do anything I don't want to," Katrin answered. Then she leaned forward and added the words that would haunt him until the final time he saw her: "Just so you know, Elpenor, this has nothing to do with the laundry."

Katrin wasn't alone in objecting to the miracle washers. When Jeff returned from lunch the following afternoon, he found Timon Demopolis leaning against the change machine and chain-smoking volcanically. The owner of the Kwick Wash displayed a six figure cashier's check. He reminded Jeff of the sweepstakes winners on television—only the Greek wasn't smiling. *We do equal partners*, said Demopolis. *Sixty me, forty you.* To Jeff's amazement, he even gave up smoking when asked—albeit, by tossing his lit cigarette onto the linoleum and letting it smolder until Jeff crushed it under his shoe. *Maybe your machines are contagious,* said the Greek. *We move a few to my place and mine do miracles as well.* His every other phrase ended with *my dear friend* or *my dear young man.* Only later, when Jeff rejected his "final" *fifty-five, forty-five* offer, did the Greek resort to such phrases as *You cock-sucking faggot* and *I'll grind your nuts to shavings and gouge them into your eyes.*

Demopolis merely threatened. The Filipino couple acted. They must have cashed in all of their chips at city hall because every day brought another official inspection. The Health Department cited Jeff for mold in his storage room. The Buildings Department gave him thirty days to rewire. His "No Smoking" signs proved too small; his aisles weren't wide enough for wheelchairs. Doc Happy accidentally overturned a bucket during a visit by the state's environmental authorities and they wrote Jeff up for improperly disposing laundry water. He even managed to run afoul of several left-wingers at the attorney general's office in Albany who were threatening him with prosecution for unjust enrichment and mail fraud. But what really got to him were the private law suits from unsatisfied customers: One from a prematurely bald rabbinical student whose hair hadn't grown back, another from a Dominican woman who lived above the store and claimed his machines were interfering with her psychic powers.

And then there was Katrin. So complex, so everything. They spent all of their time—except the hours supervising their respective laundries—together. They made excursions to the pier at Orchard Beach (where Katrin taught him to haggle for fresh fish) and to the Peekskill farmer's market (where she showed him how to select the ripest watermelons). She told him about Holland: the Sunday marriages at the Haarlem Kerk, the newlywed aristocrats releasing hundreds of white doves. He told stories of endless twilights on Cormorant Island, of flocks of spoonbills, pink and gentle, like birthday gifts for a hundred baby girls. Sometimes they discussed classics: Virgil, Ovid. But mostly just in passing. He often feared that she thought he knew more than he did. To tell the truth, he didn't quite understand what she saw in him. He asked her once and she answered: "Everybody has their burdens to bear, Elpenor,"—and then she squeezed his crotch through his jeans. If Jeff's washing machines hadn't reunited seventy-three year old Mrs. Goldwasser and her high school sweetheart, or helped Mrs. Gates to lose forty pounds, his life with Katrin would have been truly magical.

Jeff did not know what to do. Part of his difficulty was that he'd come to view The Magic Laundry as a public service. Whether through actual wizardry or some mass placebo effect, his machines had improved—were improving—the lives of hundreds of people. Strangers baked him pies, invited him to weddings. His father was finally off his case. What was more, now that Doc Happy had learned the ropes, Jeff had ample time to wade through Catullus and to visit the indoor batting cage. And hadn't he rinsed his clothes in a magic washer on the night of his first date with Katrin? Could this all be *so* wrong? But it *did* feel wrong, especially when Election Day rolled past and the Segovia's pinned a sign on their gate reading: "Out of Business—God's Will."

Jeff walked past Madame Ursula's several times—on the opposite side of the street, striding quickly—and he was stunned to see the place desolate. Katrin sat atop the safe, reading. Her aunt moved nervously at the window, sitting down, then standing up, like a debutante being stood up for a ball. Katrin never spoke to Jeff about her business woes. Still, they clouded his every hour. During his junior year at Columbia, a male friend had confided in Jeff that the guy's girlfriend was pregnant and that, despite his pleading, she didn't want to have an abortion. The couple fought bitterly, every night. Still, they continued to date. They kept dating and arguing all the way through the first trimester. And then they stopped speaking about the fetus, ignored it as it grew ever larger on its journey to babyhood. This, thought Jeff, was like that.

One afternoon, while strolling on the plaza behind Grant's Tomb, he made the mistake of suggesting that he'd be willing to support Katrin—to support all the Luczaks—if she went to graduate school.

"Fuck you," she said.

Jeff stopped walking. "What's that supposed to mean?"

"Do you want it in Greek?"

Jeff was suddenly conscious of other pedestrians: an elderly man with brittle knees walking an arthritic terrier, two overweight teenage girls jogging. "Look," said Jeff. "I was just trying to be helpful."

"I told you," said Katrin, stiffly. "Nobody ever makes me do anything I don't want to do. *This*—you and me—had absolutely nothing to do with *that.*"

Jeff looked away. Nearby, a muscular kid in a flannel shirt was displaying his skateboarding skills for his girlfriend. Jeff feared arguing. He said: "Of course, it does."

"Fine, it does," Katrin answered. "Have it your way."

Her words were ambiguous. "So you'll let me help you out?"

The wind picked up and sliced into Jeff's back. He wanted to hug Katrin for warmth—to squeeze away their fight—but she stood too far away.

"You have to stop," she said. "It's fraud. It's taking advantage of people. It's total bullshit. If you want to run a laundry the way other honest people do—and God knows why the fuck you would—that's your prerogative. But I'm telling you, you are going to stop." Katrin tugged on the hood strings of her sweatshirt. "I love you, Elpenor. But I love me more."

"Okay," said Jeff. "I'll think about it."

"Okay," said Katrin. "You'd better."

That evening they had great sex and then Katrin told him about how she'd read that, as children, both Tom Brokaw and Dan Rather had ridden in electric dryers for fun. They laughed late into the night. Though they didn't talk about the laundry business per se, they didn't *not* talk about it as they'd been doing for nearly two months. Jeff's world seemed rich with enchantment. But he woke up, during the cavernous hours of the early morning, with renewed dread. He looked over at Katrin, sleeping: How helpless her face appeared nestled in the pillow, how unlike the strong-willed, intense scamp of the daylight. Jeff eased his body out of bed and retrieved her jeans and t-shirt from the carpet. It was worth a shot, he thought—and he would be doing it *for her.* If anyone deserved a miracle, he told himself, it was Katrin. What he was doing might be devious, even a bit presumptuous, but not actually wrong.

When Jeff returned from the laundromat, his bed was empty. He checked to see if Katrin had gone off in the dress she'd given him on their first date, or maybe in one of his own shirts, but his closet and bureaus appeared undisturbed. She must have left in her underwear, he thought. Walked three city blocks in her underwear! Jeff considered phoning the police, but didn't. Too much explaining. What he wanted to do was to call Katrin at home to beg forgiveness, at that very moment, but he knew to wait until morning. Instead he pondered her daring, half-naked escape: Secretly, against his wishes, he found it breathtakingly sexy.

Jeff had no advance warning, no call from the police. He climbed down the front steps the following morning, like any other, the dawn just nipping over the elevated tracks. He passed his corner bodega and decided against buying a newspaper. At 119th Street, he noticed a blue police cordon and yellow crime tape. It couldn't be Katrin, he thought. It just couldn't. But at the corner of 118th and Broadway, he realized that it wasn't. It was the laundry. Charred, gutted—her front split open like the jaws of a rotting beast. Several passersby had congregated at a safe distance: Mrs. Garcia's two squat friends, a one-armed black man carrying a stack of books under the other. Jeff gazed helplessly into the rubble that had once housed Douglas Fairbanks and Rudolph Valentino until a female investigator from the arson squad insisted upon asking him questions about his property insurance. He vacantly mentioned Demopolis' threats; no arrests were ever made.

That afternoon Jeff received a polite hand-delivered note from Madame Ursula, sympathizing with his loss and offering him the post of general manager at her laundry. He never answered it. Instead, he joined his father in the dental equipment business. Eventually, his firm supplied articulating paper to nearly all of the dentists in Florida.

The House Call

For several topsy-turvy years after my ex-husband abandoned me to middle age, I had cancer on Mondays and Thursdays. One spring it was a bladder tumor that made urinating frequent and painful; later, I suffered from something called an oat cell carcinoma, which sprouted in my lungs and then slithered its way into my brain and my femurs. Yet for most of my half-decade as a patient at the Havilland Center, my problem was a malignant mass inside my pancreas with a prognosis grimmer than being struck by lightning. I was only forty-eight years old, but I was going to die. You can't imagine what it felt like gorging myself on Fudgesicles and Mallomars at the hospital cafeteria, waiting for my checkup, all the while knowing that I'd never survive to see my daughters graduate from high school—that I'd never find out how Dynasty concluded or whether Bush or Dukakis would be elected President. But that's exactly what I was supposed to do: Internalize Harriet Steinhoff's suffering so deeply that the medical students who interviewed me genuinely believed that I was a widowed Connecticut homemaker dying of an abdominal disease, rather than a divorced actress who needed the two hundred dollars per session to make the payments on her Yonkers condo. That was the part I was best at. Being Harriet. Sobbing over wallet photos of Amanda and Alyssa, my perpetually seventeen year old twins. I suppose personal tragedy has always been my strongest suit. The challenge for me was the grading. On any given day at the Havilland Center, there were eight simulated patients demanding various forms of assistance—a teenager in need of prenatal counseling, a blind diabetic at odds with her home health aide, a retired architect who had to be told he had Alzheimer's. Burl Vincent, who played the architect, had once toured regionally as "Professor" Harold Hill in *The Music Man;* he'd been losing his memory for the medical students twice each week since 1978. The ingénues portraying the pregnant girl never lasted more than a month; either they landed roles on a more conventional stage, or they quit the acting life entirely. We all worked along a corridor of adjacent mock-examination rooms on the ninth floor of Hudson Hospital, where Oscar Havilland, the pork-chop-baron-turned-healthcare-philanthropist, had once been treated for liver failure. The medical students came from Columbia and N.Y.U and Mount Sinai, from as far away as Pittsburgh and Providence. The schools paid a fortune to have their skills assessed. My assignment was to evaluate these future physicians on a series of highly-defined tasks: Did they explain the causes of pancreatic tumors in clear, easily-understood language? Did they express appropriate compassion? Did they wash their hands before and after the encounter? I never did figure out what distinguished "OUTSTANDING" hand-washing from scrubbing that was merely "VERY GOOD"—nor did I particularly care—which is why I was constantly reprimanded for marking too generously.

It didn't help any that the students were Zachary's age. Or I suppose I should say the age that Zachary *would have been*, because my son remains frozen at fourteen forever. So how could I pass judgment upon anybody else's child? Year after year, my grades drifted higher. I awarded two OUSTANDINGS for each EXCELLENT, then twenty-one OUTSTANDINGS in a row. The director of the Havilland Center, Dr. Fishberg, pleaded with me to elevate my standards; later, she resorted to an official warning on letterhead. Eventually, the Board of Directors hired a pair of statistical consultants from Johns Hopkins, and I was asked to clear out my locker. Not that I minded very much. By then, I was also subbing as a kindergarten teacher, and earning enough to pay my bills, so I let Burl Vincent take me out to a farewell lunch at Pastarnack's Delicatessen, and I put my cancer days behind me. That was the spring I turned fifty. Another decade would pass before my tumor emerged from remission.

~

My son is buried alongside his grandfather in a sprawling, soulless Jewish cemetery just north of Interstate 287. The second grave had once been destined for my mother, but Mom's second husband subsequently purchased plots in Broward County, Florida—walking distance to the beach, he liked to boast—which meant we had a spare for emergencies. When

Robert and I were still together, we visited Zachary each year on his birthday, but after Bob left me, I made a point of visiting one week late so that I wouldn't risk crossing paths with him. The truth was that Zachary's death hadn't destroyed our marriage. It had nearly saved it. Overnight, we'd gone from running on fumes to running on grief—we stuck it out for another decade, mainly out of misplaced loyalty to Zach—and then I guess Robert finally exhausted his share of the heartbreak. I didn't even hate him for it. But there's not much you can say to a man you've slept next to for twenty-three years, and buried a son with, that won't leave you feeling hostile or lonely, so I pretended April 4th was a date like any other. A few days afterward, if the skies looked clear and I wasn't called in to teach, I'd ride the county bus out to White Plains, switch lines at Elmsford, and hike the last half mile from the Chatham depot to the gates of the King Solomon Cemetery. Zachary had always given me the hardest time for never learning how to drive—I was the only mother in his grade who couldn't carpool—but I hadn't found it much of a hardship, not even living in the suburbs, and on balmy spring afternoons, it sometimes felt like a blessing.

The cemetery hardly changed in the twenty years after we lost Zachary, but the environs developed quickly. Subdivisions and a twelve-screen multiplex replaced acres of horse pasture and berry orchard. Caterpillar bulldozers razed hills and filled ponds to create adjoining golf courses, one municipal and one private. For many people, I realize, that's progress—but I'm too old for that sort of progress. To my thinking, action films and cocktails at the nineteenth hole are no substitute for the melody of songbirds. So I was genuinely delighted when I embarked upon my pilgrimage to the graveyard last spring, ten years to the month since I'd left the Havilland Center, and I discovered that a mom & pop plant nursery had opened cattycorner to the hulking movie house. Out front, sawhorse tables displayed tightly-packed azaleas and peonies, as well as a wonderland of empty terracotta pots. Two low-slung greenhouses, pregnant with the rich honeyed-air of the tropics, offered up rows of exotic succulents. A spruce-raftered warehouse stored phalanxes of leaf-blowers and lawnmowers. Behind these structures, and extending as far as the first stand of oversized ranch homes, a small farm nurtured bell peppers and pattypan squash and pole beans winding around trellises. Okay, it was more of a vegetable patch than a genuine farm, but it brought me joy to look at.

The unlikely farmers were a pair of Korean-born tax lawyers with heavy Brooklyn accents, Sammy and Shelly Go, who'd quit the corporate life in their forties. I learned all this from eavesdropping while I browsed bouquets for Zachary. But then I sensed that the young woman who'd been chatting with Mr. and Mrs. Go was looking at me—staring at me—and I feared that I'd been too conspicuous.

I picked up an African violet—for effect—and examined the price tag. Then I glanced casually at my watch. The woman continued to stare. She was a short, small-framed creature with a chest as flat as a twelve-year-old boy's, and *de rigeur* sunglasses propped in her highlighted burgundy hair, but she also had large, kind eyes and a soft smile. She couldn't have been much more than thirty, maybe thirty-five. And she was gazing at me as though she recognized me—as though *I* should recognize *her*, too. My first instinct was that she might have been a friend of Zach's from school, one of those scores of teens who'd sent nearly identical cards and had sobbed puddles at the funeral. I had no memory of having met her.

"Mrs. Steinhoff?" she asked. "Is that really you?"

She smiled at me innocently, but I felt like a spy whose cover had been blown by a chance run-in with an old acquaintance. Nobody had ever before—or since—called me by my simulated-patient name outside the hospital.

"I'm Jeannie Ballard," she said in a fast, almost breathless voice. The girl balanced a paper shopping bag on her tiny hip; her pocketbook dangled off her elbow. "You don't remember me, do you? I was one of the second-year medical students from Yale who met with you at that place…."

"The Havilland Center," I offered.

"That's right," she said. "The Havilland Center. God, that was a long time ago." Jeannie Ballard looked wistful, vulnerable. Somehow, she'd resisted that varnish of benevolent detachment that renders most doctors capable of infinite sympathy, but not empathy. I was pleased to see this—that she'd lived up to her "OUTSTANDING." She kept her eyes focused on me, examining, but gently, and if we hadn't been separated by vast trays of pansies and begonias, I suspect she would have placed her small hand on my elbow. Instead, she lowered her voice and asked, as a concerned friend might, "Have you been okay?" She paused nervously, and added, "I know that sounds silly, but I was never really sure…."

I nodded. "It's a pleasure to meet you, Jeannie," I said. "But my real name's not Harriet Steinhoff. It's Miriam Littman."

"Of course," she agreed. "Miriam."

But she looked surprised that I wasn't Harriet. I took this as a compliment.

"You were *so* convincing," she said. "I really believed you were dying."

"That's very kind of you to say," I said. "Harriet was my favorite role."

Jeannie lifted the paper bag from her hip and rested it on a corner of the sawhorse. "I always wondered how much of what you told us was true. I mean, I know you didn't have pancreatic cancer….How could you have?....But did you really have daughters in high school and a ninety-eight-year-old grandmother who'd once worked with Madame Curie?"

I'd forgotten all about my grandmother in the nursing home—an unauthorized flourish that I'd inserted into Harriet's back-story. It amazed me that Jeannie Ballard still recalled the details of our brief encounter so thoroughly, that she remembered how Grandma Steinhoff had helped to isolate radium. She'd probably seen thousands of patients since then. Maybe tens of thousands. I flattered myself that I was one of the most memorable—and not merely one of the first. I hated to disappoint her with the truth.

"Let's just say it wasn't *all* untrue," I answered. "My grandmother *was* French and she *was* a chemist, but she didn't work with the Curies. And I had a son, not daughters."

"Well, you had me totally convinced," she said.

"Thank you again." I realized that I had to ask about her life too, even though I was in no psychological state for chitchat. "And you, dear? How is the world of medicine?"

"Good enough. I'm buying Christmas tree lights," she said. "My older son's in fifth grade and he's building a diorama about Indian Tribes—his father's brilliant idea—so I've been running from store to store all afternoon looking for Christmas tree lights. You don't want to know what it's like trying to find Christmas tree lights in April."

"But you found them?"

"Only the clear ones. Not the colored ones. But he'll survive."

"I'm sure he will," I said.

He'll survive. How many times had I uttered the same words about Zachary? How many scraped knees and missing lacrosse sticks and bouts of puppy-love had I predicted he'd survive? Because most boys do. Nearly all of them do. That's what the therapist had assured us, after his first bout of moping. Yet once in a while there's a child too sensitive for his own good—what mathematics professors like my ex-husband term an outlier—and then surviving loses some of its inevitability. Robert and Zachary had also built a diorama for school once: The Battle of Lexington and Concord. Patriots in the foreground, Redcoats marching lockstep in the distance. The best damn diorama Mrs. Pelican's fourth grade had ever seen. I didn't mention any of this to Jeannie Ballard. Even I recognized that gloating about your dead son's fourth grade history project rarely endears you to casual acquaintances.

I sensed the tears welling behind my eyes.

"Well, it was nice running into you," I said.

"Absolutely," said Jeannie Ballard. She appeared as though she wanted to say something more—even to offer me a parting hug—but she didn't. "Good luck with everything."

I turned away quickly and scooped up the first marginally-suitable flower I could find, a solitary blood-red Oriental poppy. Mrs. Go gave me a 25% discount: "Because you're a returning customer—You just don't know it yet."

~

Outside the nursery, a conclave of grackles rummaged through the crabgrass at the curbside and, farther out of the public golf course, Canada geese preened their rigid necks. The breeze had picked up, rustling the hemlock hedge. Puffs of friendly clouds played peek-a-boo with the afternoon sun. I'd already put a good fifty yards between myself and the plant shop, thinking about Zachary, about what had become of that Lexington & Concord diorama, when Jeannie Ballard's minivan drew up alongside me. The power window descended slowly. Like a guillotine in reverse.

"Need a lift?" she asked.

I didn't. I wanted solitude. But I also didn't wish to be overtly rude. I dug deep into my actor's trick-bag for a plausible pretext to decline her offer, but came up empty-handed. "I'm not going very far," I pleaded anemically. "Just up the street."

"Nonsense," she insisted. "Hop in."

The inside of the minivan was cluttered with children's galoshes, and library books, and a tomb of crushed soda cans in the compartment behind the gearshift. An air-freshener hung from the rearview mirror, masking the scents of daily living under lemon-pine. Photos of Jeannie's sons, freckled kids with big ears, were taped to the glove-box door. On the passenger seat lay a physician's white coat and a stethoscope. Jeannie cleared them away so that I could sit down.

"Do you make house calls?" I asked.

"Those are Campbell's," she answered, rolling her eyes. "My younger one went dressed as a doctor for Halloween, and now he insists on wearing his costume everywhere. We have a deal that he can take it with him on the way to school, but he has to leave it in the car." Jeannie Ballard folded the small white coat and tucked it under the armrest. She eased the minivan back into traffic, and asked, "Now where are you headed?"

Not to the cemetery, I suddenly realized. Not see to Zach. I'd come back again the next day—on my own—once I'd had time to recalibrate myself. So that meant I was headed home to Yonkers. I braced the poppy blossom between my knees. "Could you drop me in front of the train station?" I asked. "I can catch my bus there."

"I'm not letting you take the bus anywhere," answered Jeannie. She grinned. "You are a ten-year pancreatic cancer survivor, after all. There aren't too many of those around."

"Well, I live in Yonkers, but—"

"Yonkers, here we come."

She made a U-turn at a service station and pulled onto the state highway. It was already approaching rush hour and the traffic was heavy. "The boys have karate on Tuesdays," she said. "They spend Tuesday nights with their father."

So we both belonged to the jilted spouse's club! But Jeannie Ballard had earned her membership early; she might yet have other opportunities ahead of her.

"Are you still acting?" she asked.

"Now and then," I answered. "I do some summer stock."

The truth was that I hadn't done summer-stock in several years. Compared to portraying Harriet Steinhoff, where I'd always been the star of my own one-woman show, there wasn't much luster in playing a Scottish townswoman in Brigadoon or a pirate's wife in Peter Pan. But I sensed that I was shortchanging Jeannie Ballard's expectations once again—first as a patient and now as an actress—so something must have gone haywire with my moral compass, because I said, "To be honest, I haven't had much energy for theater since the chemotherapy."

"Chemotherapy?" asked Jeannie Ballard.

"Not pancreatic cancer," I explained. "Just a small oat cell tumor in my lung. And maybe a bit of it in my brain and femurs."

Jeannie glanced at me—devastated. It had slipped my mind that she was a physician, that she knew the prognosis of oat-cell metastases. I feared that I'd gone too far.

"I'll be fine," I added quickly. "I'm in remission now. I'm very lucky."

"Oh, that's wonderful news," said Jeannie. "About the remission, I mean." She reached over and touched my elbow with her tiny fingers. "I'm sorry you've had to go through all that."

"It hasn't been as bad as you might think," I said. "I suppose playing Harriet Steinhoff all those years prepared me for the worst of it."

Then I narrated the rollercoaster course of my illness—coughing up blood on my fifty-fifth birthday, radiation, chemo, more chemo, fighting insurers who refused to pay for bone scans—pausing only to offer driving directions. I don't know why I did it. I could have told Jeannie Ballard about how my teenage son went out one Saturday night and intentionally stepped in front of a commuter train—or stumbled in front of it accidentally, because nobody will ever know for certain—and how I spent the next six months, lying in bed, cataloguing every infinitesimal mistake I'd made over the course of fourteen years. That's a story far more horrific than any personal illness, even an aggressive lung carcinoma. Even sudden death. But after all those years playing Harriet Steinhoff, it was easier to tell her story than my own.

"You're a very brave woman," said Jeannie. "I can hear it in your voice."

"I just play my part," I answered. "I sometimes second-guess myself about all those years at the Havilland Center. Because I never made it to Broadway. *Or television.* I hardly even did much community theater. But running into a practicing physician like you who I helped to train—even in the smallest way—makes all that time seem worthwhile." That part was true. Seeing Jeannie did make me feel useful. I could tell she was listening to me—unlike my own doctor, a dour Jordanian man with the bedside manner of a cigar store Indian. "You must make a wonderful physician, Jeannie. Your patients must be extremely fortunate to have you."

I wished I hadn't lied about the tumor. I'd gladly have ditched the Jordanian for her any day, even if it meant an increased copayment.

"Thank you," answered Jeannie. "You should never think twice about your work at the Havilland Center. Mrs. Steinhoff was the best first patient anybody could ever have asked for."

We rode several minutes in silence. I gazed out the passenger window at the passing strip malls, the banners advertising "Spring-Cleaning Sales" and boosting the local girls' softball team. It struck me that if Zachary had lived, he might have married a woman a lot like Jeannie Ballard. *He might have married Jeannie Ballard.*

"Do you have a specialty?" I asked.

She looked up, startled—as though she'd also been lost in thought. I already regretted my question. I hoped to God that she wouldn't say oncology.

"Not exactly," she answered. "I never made it that far in my training."

"Well, I'm glad you're not a specialist," I said. "Too many specialists these days. Not enough old-fashioned internists anymore."

I had intended this to be supportive, but Jeannie's hands started to tremble. Before I knew what had happened, she was sobbing violently.

"I'm not a doctor," she said. "There, I said it. Okay? I'm not a doctor."

I don't think her words could have been more unnerving, more downright shocking, if she'd announced them while standing over my operating table. I feared for a moment that she might hyperventilate—even that she might drive off the road—but she took several deep breaths and composed herself rapidly. "I'm not a physician," she said again—matter-of-fact. "I'm sorry I've I led you to believe otherwise."

"It's all right, honey," I assured her.

"No it's not all right," she said. "It's just how things turned out."

"Because of the children?" I asked.

Jeannie shook her head. "Long before that. I didn't even finish the second year of med school. Actually, it was that afternoon at the Havilland Center that did me in. I remember having to tell that nice old man that he had Alzheimer's, and then there was the college student who could never have children, and you with your pancreatic cancer—and I realized I didn't have it in me. I could handle the long hours and the endless studying….but the sadness was too much for me. I know that must sound ridiculous, but I just couldn't go through with it. Or maybe I could have, but I didn't know it at the time…."

"It's never too late," I suggested.

"It's too late. Trust me," answered Jeannie. "Do you know what I do for a living now? I babysit for dead people." She smiled—but it was a bitter smile. "Mortuaries hire me to go sit in wealthy dead people's homes while their families attend funerals, so that burglars can't take advantage of the tragic circumstances. It turns out that even burglars read the obituaries….I bet you didn't even know a job like mine existed."

I didn't. "But you have your boys," I said.

Jeannie smiled. "That's right. I have my boys. Without them….I don't know what…."

Of course she didn't. Who did? I ran my fingers over the petals of the poppy blossom, tracing the thin veins of life to their roots. I suddenly realized that I wouldn't return to the King Solomon Cemetery the next morning, or the morning after that. Or maybe ever. That I'd played my part already and I was ready for another role.

"Sometimes I meet people like you—with cancer I mean—or Alzheimer's, or Parkinson's, or even just pneumonia—and I wish so much I could help them." Jeannie sighed. She retrieved a tissue from a cup-holder and wiped the stained eye-liner from her cheeks. "I would honestly do anything to help you, Miriam. If I could."

That's how far we'd gotten when the minivan pulled up in front of my condo. Several young children played on the front steps under the watchful eyes of their nannies. Squirrels darted friskily around the KEEP OFF THE GRASS signs. Across the street, a team of men in white undershirts blasted Latin music while unloading crates of bananas from a box truck. An ordinary, truly unremarkable suburban afternoon. Jeannie Ballard didn't say anything else, she just reached over the gear shift and squeezed my hand. Her touch was reassuring, therapeutic. For a brief moment, I let myself believe that if she'd been a real doctor, and I'd actually had cancer, she'd have been able to heal me.

The Empress Of Charcoal

The note arrived on Yale University letterhead, neatly typed, three years to the month after she'd lost her husband:

May 15, 20—

Dear Elsa,

I imagine you don't remember me. I was a student in Professor Stanley's figure drawing class at City College during the spring semester of 1962, when you served as a model. After the course ended, I asked the Visual Arts Department for your name, but I didn't have the courage to contact you. I suppose you will think me foolish—and no doubt I am—but that remains among the greatest regrets of my adult life. My wife of thirty-six years passed away last August and my son helped me find your address on the Internet. Would you be willing to have lunch one of these days?

Sincerely,
Morton D. Belldauer, Ph.D.
Professor Emeritus
Department of the History of Mathematics

PS: If you are not the same Elsa Kalamaransky who modeled at City College in 1962, kindly disregard this message.

Elsa was not the same woman who had modeled for Professor Stanley's class. She'd already been teaching five years at Bonneville by 1962, initiating her girls into the marvels of Balzac and Flaubert. But ever since the balmy, cloudless morning when she'd discovered Bruce facedown in his beloved Jacuzzi, skin bloated and puckered like a bobbing apple, springtime tormented Elsa with its insincere promise. It was during one of her lonely spells that she replied to Belldauer in longhand:

Dear Morton,

What a delightful surprise! I confess I do not remember you, but 1962 was an eternity ago, wasn't it? My life here in Rhode Island has been a good one. As Emily Dickinson wrote, "To live is so startling it leaves little time for anything else." I retired six years ago from teaching at The Bonneville School, shortly after it merged with an all-boys academy. At the end, I was teaching only French language, but I was initially hired as an instructor of Italian literature as well. Are you a fan of Leopardi? I do hope so.

As of now, the summer is surprisingly open. My late husband (39 years together, 3 apart) was an avid gardener, and although I fear I lack his natural gifts, I'm doing my darnedest to keep my thumbs green. I believe I can claim some success, as this weekend the peonies are staging a wondrous show.

Please do come see the daylilies while they are in bloom.

Most warmly,

Elsa Kalamaransky

She reread the letter twice before sealing it inside the envelope, unsure if she'd included too much or too little. She'd been one of six sisters, and all of her life she'd worked among women, so what little she understood of men came from interacting with Bruce and his colleagues in the Providence Philharmonic—not, most likely, a representative sampling of the species. At the central post office in Creve Coeur, she tore open the envelope to verify that she'd printed the correct telephone number beneath her signature, and she had to purchase a replacement at the counter.

Elsa sent the letter on Saturday morning. Belldauer phoned in the early evening on Wednesday, and now it was Saturday again, and she was expecting him at noon. "At my age, I don't like to put anything off," he'd joked in a voice as deep and resonant as a kettle drum. "Besides, the way I see it, I'm already forty-five years overdue." Elsa had expected him to sound more patrician, less ethnic Brooklyn—like Cary Grant without the effeminate tinge. But the professor did come across as very much the gentleman. Bruce, rest his soul, had been a slow-spoken tenor with an accent to shame the Kennedys.

She'd started planning their meal the evening that Belldauer phoned and, in hindsight, she'd gone a bit overboard: After all, he was a stranger who'd been sweet on her nearly half a century ago. Not even *on her*. *On a woman who had shared her name!* But Elsa had endured so long without cause to indulge, that now she couldn't resist a drive to the gourmet supermarket in Providence for fresh Bluefin tuna and hand-picked Nyons olives. She tossed the tuna in a homegrown spinach salad. Then she covered the wrought-iron table in the garden with her late mother-in-law's daisy-print cloth. As lunchtime approached and the skies remained clear, she set out a basket of assorted breads, a porcelain platter of camembert and brie, and the swan-shaped glass water pitcher that her wealthy grand-aunt had bestowed upon her and Bruce as a wedding gift. All night long, a driving rain had pummeled the neighborhood, forcing Elsa to reassess her plans, but by Friday morning, the air had turned crisp with potential. On the slate patio, puddles shimmered under the high white sun.

Belldauer's car—a dignified jet-black Oldsmobile—pulled up at the curb ten minutes early, but the professor waited inside the vehicle until precisely twelve. Elsa watched through the bay windows in the living room as he advanced up the front path and paused under the crabapple tree to adjust the sleeves of his sports jacket. He was trim and long-limbed, with a grand forehead and a bushy, salt-and-pepper mustache. The mustache, reflected Elsa, might take some adjusting to. Otherwise, Belldauer was as handsome as any man she'd laid eyes upon—at least, since that distant night when Rachel Kalamaransky, her colleague at Bonneville, had invited Elsa backstage at the symphony to meet her unmarried and "pleasantly eccentric" brother. The professor even carried himself rather like Bruce, his magnificent head cocked slightly skyward, as he stepped onto the front porch, holding his bouquet of lilacs. How fortunate that she'd had the nerve to write back! Then her chest fluttered with second thoughts: What if he realized she was the wrong Elsa? What if he didn't, but rejected her when she later confessed? What if the other Elsa Kalamaransky had been significantly less busty? Or black? Or an achondroplastic dwarf? When the doorbell chimed, she found herself paralyzed with anxiety. After a pause, the bell rang again. Elsa clenched her eyelids together, as though she were about to dive into a pool of icy water, and she crossed briskly through the foyer to welcome her guest.

The portico stood a step down from the entryway, so when Elsa opened the door, she and Belldauer faced each other at eye level. He said nothing, at first. For half a second, he just stared at her, his brow furrowed as though reconstructing a puzzle in his mind from memory. And then he flashed her a broad grin. "Goodness, Elsa Kalamaransky," he said. "It's really you, isn't it?"

"Please, come inside," answered Elsa. "I'm so glad you're here."

Soon they were standing in the parlor, surrounded by upholstery and knickknacks, and again he was examining her. She accepted the lilacs from his outstretched hand and her gaze followed his nervously around the room. Photos of her long life with Bruce cluttered the piano bench and the end tables, including several from their first honeymoon in the Canadian Rockies, and now Elsa regretted not having moved them upstairs.

"Did you have an easy drive?" asked Elsa.

"Oh, it was fine. I just can't believe it's actually you," said Belldauer. "The Empress of Charcoal, in the flesh."

"Excuse me?"

"That's what I used to call you. The Empress of Charcoal," he explained. "I suspect you'll laugh at me if I tell you why…."

"Try me," answered Elsa. She felt herself growing confident, even flirtatious. "But first, let's head onto the veranda. As far as I'm concerned, it's far too lovely an afternoon to squander another moment out of the sun."

She took hold of the professor's hand and led him through the sliding glass doors. Belldauer's skin felt warm to her touch. Outside, on the low-hanging branches of the Japanese maple, a pair of orioles serenaded each other; from beyond the forsythia hedge rose the cries of the neighbor's children, and the occasional blast of a firecracker. Elsa tucked Belldauer's lilacs into her plastic watering jug and centered the bouquet atop the gas grill. Bruce had enjoyed hosting barbecues for his fellow musicians, but ever since she'd lost him, Elsa used the device as a sideboard. "Now where were we?" asked Elsa, smiling coyly. "Oh, yes. I was about to laugh at your story."

"I wouldn't blame you," said the professor. "As I was saying, the office adjacent to Dr. Stanley's belonged to the chairman of the history department. Big, meaty fellow—I've forgotten his name. In any case, the two of them shared one of those long glass-enclosed bulletin boards, and Stanley used to post our charcoal sketches next to this pictorial genealogy chart of the royal houses of Europe. So one afternoon, I was standing in the corridor, looking over the various ways the class had portrayed you, and somehow 'The Empress of Charcoal' popped into my head. Foolish, no?"

"Not in the slightest," said Elsa. "May I offer you a drink?"

"It's only noon. I wouldn't want to give you the wrong impression."

"Nonsense," she retorted. "I still have a pitcher of frozen banana daiquiri left over from my niece's birthday picnic. How about I pour us each a glass and then I give you a walking tour of the garden?"

"I never say no to a lady," answered Belldauer. "Or to a chilled cocktail."

Elsa retrieved the crystal decanter from the mini-fridge and filled two cognac glasses. She'd prepared the contents the evening before, several weeks *after* her niece's birthday celebration, but it was a harmless lie. The truth was that she hardly drank at all—champagne on New Year's, Manischewitz at her sister-in-law's Passover dinner, an occasional Bloody Mary at a wedding or shower—but she didn't want Belldauer to think her puritanical. Secretly, she also hoped to limber up his judgment.

"Here's mud in your eye!" she declared. "To second chances!"

They clinked glasses and she drank.

"It's amazing how you expect something to turn out one way, and it works out so differently, yet it's still just as good," said Belldauer.

"What do you mean?"

"It's hard to explain." He sipped from his glass. "I still remember how stunning you looked that first afternoon when you slid that Japanese dressing gown off your shoulders, and all you were wearing was that startling blue bracelet around your wrist....For some reason, I expected you to be reserved, aloof....and you're so friendly."

"I suppose I might have come across as aloof *back then,*" said Elsa. "I can pretend to be less friendly, if you'd prefer." She sensed the heat of the daiquiri in her temples. "Or even downright mean."

"That won't be necessary," said Belldauer, beaming. "I have a strange confession to make. After I wrote to you, I still wasn't sure that I'd have it in me to meet you face-to-face. I'd be lying if I didn't admit that I miss Louise. Like hell, I miss Louise. Every day. I'll be reading a book or listening to the radio and my mind begins drifting to what she looked like during those final nights at the hospice. Of course, my son—he's a headshrinker at Johns Hopkins—assures me it will get better....."

Bullshit, thought Elsa. It might be *different,* but never better. She still woke up every morning, three years later, shocked not to find Bruce, his paunch poking over his boxers, hogging the pillows onto his side of the bed.

Elsa squeezed Belldauer's wrist. "Poor dear," she said.

"Honestly, I wasn't thinking too clearly when I sent you that note," he continued. "I had no idea what I'd do next—whether I'd even follow up at all. But do you know what sealed the deal for me?"

"What?"

"That you'd kept your maiden name." The professor shrugged. "I know that sounds ridiculous, but I liked that you were still a Kalamaransky."

"Why couldn't Kalamaransky be my husband's name?"

"I did the math when I received your letter. If you've been married thirty-nine years and widowed three, you were still single when you posed for us....It makes a man wonder....Had I only written to you then...." Belldauer allowed this idea to drift unfinished into the azaleas. "I've always been vehemently opposed to women changing their names when they get married," he said. "It's a particularly retrograde practice, to be blunt, based on historical notions of wives as chattel....I'm proud to say that Louise was born a Kappelgruber and, rest her soul, she died a Kappelgruber."

Elsa wasn't sure she agreed with Belldauer about name-changing, but she found endearing the vehemence with which he voiced his opinion. "Are you ready for a stroll around the yard?" she asked. "Before the morning glories and the portulaca close up shop for the afternoon?"

Elsa topped off Belldauer's drink and passed it back to him.

"And on the subject of math, Mr. Professor Emeritus at Yale University, maybe you could tell me about the variety of mathematics you studied."

"*History* of mathematics," Belldauer corrected her.

Elsa polished off her second daiquiri. "*History* of mathematics," she echoed. "Twice as impressive."

She reached for his hand again, this time clasping it more decisively, and steered him between the neatly manicured beds of dahlias and gladiolas. Now that she'd spread store-bought bark chips around the perennials—as she'd already done for several years with the zinnias and pansies—the entire patch looked far more professional.

"Most of my work focused upon cuneiform tablets, on whether the Babylonians ever developed an authentic trigonometry," said Belldauer. "I also authored several papers on advanced functions in the Sumerian system—cubic equations, Pythagorean triples. I developed a particular expertise regarding a tablet called Plimpton 322. Truthfully, I can't imagine it would interest you in the slightest…."

"You might find yourself surprised," Elsa answered. But rather than inquire anything further about Mesopotamian numerology, she pointed out the various strains of daylilies. "This over here is Honest Abe's Beard," she said, cupping the petals of a tall blossom fringed in black. "Those two red ones behind the phlox are Emma Goldman and Alexander Berkman. What was it Goldman once said? 'I'd rather have roses on my table than diamonds on my neck.' Personally, I couldn't agree more."

"You've bred all of these yourself?"

"Heavens, no. Not *me*. Bruce." Elsa wondered if she was talking too much about her husband—but, after nearly four decades of marriage, what else was she supposed to talk about? "He played the oboe. You should have seen him: Such a large man blowing into such a tiny instrument. But his real passion wasn't music. It was cross-breeding flowers….In Bruce's study, I still have an entire filing cabinet full of daylily pedigrees that I can't make heads nor tails of. I can't bring myself to discard them…."

"Louise was a dietician," said Belldauer—reflectively, almost as though he were thinking aloud. "She worked at the university hospital."

Elsa said nothing. One of her own sisters had also been a medical dietician, specially trained to counsel renal patients, before she'd suffered a breakdown and filed for permanent disability. So the Louise Kappelgruber whom Elsa now imagined, wandering the dialysis clinic, warning diabetic truck drivers against eating foods that appeared white, looked like her own dear, hopeless Gladys. Elsa didn't mention any of this, because she wanted Belldauer to think about his wife as infrequently as possible.

They circled around the far corner of the garden—past the firewood pile, the strawberry patch, the shaded hemlock arbor where Bruce had installed a polished cedar bench. The quarter acre beyond the hemlocks, up to the stockade fence, was overgrown with oak and hickory saplings. This was also where, in a small clearing, Bruce and his brother-in-law had been attempting to restore a twenty-one foot cutty cruiser that they'd salvaged from a rummage sale. The craft's lichen-coated prow still waited for them on cement blocks, oblivious to Bruce's aneurysm, unaware that Gary and Rachel had since retired to the dry heat of Phoenix. Belldauer tapped the side of the vessel with his fingers, generating a hollow thud. "One of my former students owns a boat like this," he observed. "He takes me out on the Sound two or three times every summer." This reminded Elsa of her girls from Bonneville, all of whom were now adults, many with fully-grown children of their own. One was even a grandmother—to twins! And another, Maria Coats, was the provost at Bryn Mawr College. Elsa had many regrets in life—not having children, not spending more time with Bruce—but choosing a teaching career was never among them. She reached for Belldauer's elbow and led him further into the lush greenery, keeping her feet on the flagstones to avoid the mud.

She paused in front of Bruce's favorite lily—his prized accomplishment. The blossom wasn't *officially* blue according to the American Hemerocallis Society's standards—technically, it was aquamarine—so Bruce hadn't won their challenge award. But it was certainly blue enough to fool the average observer. "These beauties here are the Ida Kalamaransky blooms," said Elsa. *Named after Bruce's mother*, she almost added. But she caught herself in time, and blurted out, "Bruce named them after my mother." She held her breath, waiting for Belldauer to call out her lie—but he didn't. He merely smiled warmly, so Elsa leaned forward and sniffed the blossoms, more to conceal her face than to inhale the mild aroma. "Aren't they glorious?" she asked. "They always remind me of those lines from the Wordsworth poem about daffodils:

I gazed—and gazed—but little thought
What wealth the show to me had brought"

Much to Elsa's amazement, Belldauer answered:

"For oft, when on my couch I lie
In vacant or in pensive mood,
They flash upon that inward eye
Which is the bliss of solitude;
And then my heart with pleasure fills,
And dances with the daffodils."

The professor held his lapels like a ringmaster while he declaimed, clearly proud of his performance. "You look surprised," he said.

"I *am* surprised."

"Why? I'm an historian of mathematics, so I can't be cultured?"

Elsa feared she might weep from joy. "Of course, it's not that…," she answered—but at some level, it was precisely that, and in any case, she had no opportunity to present an alternative explanation. Instead, a sharp, high-pitched whistle made her look up with a start—and then a staccato of explosions sent her diving into the hollyhocks with her arms over her head. Bright sparks, orange and pink, shot from the grass around the zucchini plot. Nearby, a portion of the chicken-wire trellis collapsed, toppling with it the nascent pumpkin vines. Then Elsa's entire world turned beige as Belldauer shielded her from the blasts with his sports jacket. He stood bowed over her, like a hawk protecting its brood, and her cheek pressed against his chest.

After what seemed like months—but must have been only seconds—a deathly hush descended upon the garden. Elsa could hear her own sharp breaths and the cadence of Belldauer's heart, the two sounds merging into one complex rhythm. Then, from above, a lone catbird began trilling its chipper reveille. Elsa drew her hands away from her face and climbed out of the flower beds. The elbows of her blouse were streaked with clay, and a run slashed across the knee of her left stocking.

"What on earth was that?" she asked.

"I'd guess three or four bottle rockets," answered Belldauer. "And half a dozen cherry bombs."

"We're being bombed?"

"Firecrackers," he explained, as he dusted splinters of bark from his trousers. "It appears as though your neighbors have turned their artillery on us."

The professor stepped into the vegetable patch and poked under the chicken-wire with a jagged stick. Elsa watched anxiously as he kicked a spent rectangular canister out from the undergrowth. She wanted to warn him to be careful, but feared he would think her a worrywart. "Don't go cleaning these up on your own," said Belldauer. "Your fingers are far too adorable to risk losing. I'm afraid you'll have to ask your neighbors to call in a professional—just in case any of these shells are still active."

"I don't understand," said Elsa. "We've never had any trouble before." It figured that, on her first date in forty-two years, she'd face an armed attack. If this actually were a date, this is—and not just one-time reunion.

"They seemed like such decent boys," she added. "Their mother's a rabbi. Rabbi Bonomi. Italian Jews."

As though on cue, the Bonomi boys appeared at the break in the forsythia hedge. They were both pudgy kids with broad foreheads and impressive jaws, topped with matching shocks of auburn hair. The older youth, who could not have been much beyond ten, pushed the younger child toward Elsa and Belldauer. "My brother, Zachary," he said, "has something that he'd like to say to you."

Zachary stepped forward in increments, his eyes fixed on the damp grass.

"I'm sorry," he said—his voice soft and tentative. Elsa thought he might sob, and she felt an urge to hug him. "I did something dangerous and I'm very sorry I did it."

"Firecrackers *are* dangerous," answered Belldauer. "How old are you, Zachary?"

"Eight and seven months."

Belldauer winked at Elsa. "Do you know what I liked to do when I was eight and seven months? I liked to study the stars."

Zachary Bonomi kept his head down, his arms tucked to his chest. The older brother stepped forward and placed a reassuring hand on the boy's shoulder.

"A telescope," said Belldauer, "that's what a young *mensch* like you needs."

Elsa could sense that her date had once been an exceptional father. Speaking to these boys, he sounded as avuncular as the Wizard of Oz—only Jewish.

The professor reached into the breast pocket of his jacket. His hand emerged moments later, fingers wrapped around a short brass tube. The metal gleamed. Belldauer tugged on the cylinder and it expanded rapidly to become a foot-long telescope.

"Here you go, kid. But you shouldn't use it until the sun goes down."

The boy reached tentatively for the telescope. He peered into the broad lens, then turned the apparatus around and gazed down the narrow end.

"Can I keep it?"

"You can share it with your brother," answered Belldauer. "But on one condition. You promise not to set off any more firecrackers."

"Anywhere?" asked the boy.

"Yes," Belldauer said firmly. "*Anywhere.*"

Zachary looked to his brother for guidance. The older boy nodded.

"Okay, it's a deal," said Zachary. "Thank you."

Then the boys turned and ran, a blur of dungarees and sun-burnt flesh.

"I'm not sure what to say," said Elsa. "Do you always carry around a telescope to give to wayward schoolboys?"

"I do, in fact," answered Belldauer. "But not for wayward schoolboys. I'm rather a devotee of the night sky—it's reassuring to think that I'm seeing the same constellations as Euclid and Archimedes." He stepped back onto the path, and this time it was he who took her hand. "You'll have to decide whether you want their parents to pay to have the firecracker shells removed," he said. "I can't say I envy you that decision."

They began walking back toward the house, arm-in-arm, like a Victorian couple on a promenade through Vauxhall Gardens.

"You are certainly a man of many surprises," said Elsa. "I'm afraid to find out what else you have hidden away in those pockets of yours."

"You should be," answered Belldauer. His voice contained a new seriousness, a sense of purpose. "Let's sit down and I'll show you."

He dried off a chair for her at the lunch table and drew up his own alongside it. Then he cleared off a small square of tablecloth between the bread basket and the platters of cheese. Elsa realized what he was going to show to her at the very moment he removed the drawing from inside his coat. The sketch had been folded over many times and bore deep, irregular crease marks. One corner of the paper canvas had been shorn away entirely. In several place, the charcoal itself had streaked. But there was no mistaking the subject of Belldauer's forty-five year-old illustration. It was a young woman—a *nude* young woman—standing arms akimbo on a wooden stepladder. Fortunately, the portrait neither looked like Elsa nor unlike Elsa. Whatever his other attributes, the young Morton D. Belldauer had not been a particularly gifted sketch artist.

"I can't believe you've kept it all these years."

"I had a terrible crush on you for an entire semester," answered Belldauer. "Bear in mind, you were the first woman I'd ever seen without her clothes on."

Of course, thought Elsa. That wouldn't have been at all remarkable, back in 1962. What a different age that had been! Bruce, too, had been the first man she'd ever seen fully unclothed.

Elsa held the precious drawing as tenderly as she might hold a baby. Her hand trembled and she braced it against the tabletop. "You had talent," she observed.

"I didn't, but it's very kind of you to say so," answered Belldauer. "I've taken it up again, though. Drawing, that is. Ever since I retired from the department....I've got my art supplies in the trunk of my car."

He reached for the pitcher and poured them each a final daiquiri, shifting back and forth between glasses to ensure an equal distribution.

"I know this is going to sound crazy," said Belldauer, "but I was wondering if you'd let me draw you again...."

He sounded so innocent, so gentle. Like a fourteen-year-old schoolboy seeking permission to kiss her for the first time. The man's big dark eyes gazed into hers, brimming with tender hope, and his devotion made Elsa feel bashful. Her own eyes darted away from his quickly. Across the lawn, chipmunks scampered on the stone retaining wall opposite the cellar steps, and a dopey, overweight woodchuck sunned himself shamelessly beside the sprinkler head. She felt Belldauer's attention fixed upon her, waiting for his fate to be sealed.

"Are you serious?" Elsa asked. She had never modeled before, and she wasn't sure she'd even know how to do it. It was probably one of those feats that proved far harder than it first appeared, the sort of challenge her Bonneville girls had always relished—like drinking a gallon of whole milk in five minutes. Besides, she sensed that Belldauer had a specific sort of modeling in mind. "You don't mean...?"

"If you'd be willing. Just like in class."

"Oh, good heavens, Morton. I haven't done anything like that in years....I'm out of practice...."

"You'll do the best you can," he replied. "Let's make today the first day of your second modeling career."

"Today?"

"Today. Right here in the garden." Now Belldauer glanced away, his voice shifting to a softer, less fervent note. "I do hope I'm not offending you," he apologized. "I don't mean to put you on the spot."

"Not at all." Elsa downed what remained of her drink and rose deliberately from her chair. "Go get your supplies, Morton. I'll be back in a moment."

"Thank you," he answered.

She retreated into the house and quickly exchanged her blouse and skirt for Bruce's navy dressing gown. The silk charged her skin with desire. How unfathomable that she'd only met Morton Belldauer several hours earlier. She felt as though she'd already known him for an eternity, that the time before he'd entered her life was no longer readily accessible. Maybe this was what her Bonneville girls were feeling when they composed those essays defending Emma Bovary for having sex on a first date. Elsa assessed herself in the bedroom mirror: her rutted skin, her tired mouth, the flesh too thick between her chin and her neck. What a loon she must be, at the age of seventy-one, to compare herself to Emma Bovary. When she returned to the garden, clad only in the robe and a pair of sheepskin slippers, Belldauer had already set up his easel on the tier of flagstone across from the wishing fountain.

"You look ravishing," the professor said. "I'll never forget Dr. Stanley warning us that the models were employees hired solely to further our artistic development—that we shouldn't look upon them as women....I intended to do exactly that until the moment you walked into the studio."

Elsa scanned the perimeter of the yard. Over the years, the rhododendrons and forsythia had grown high enough to block the neighbors' view. In any case, it was her own property, wasn't it? She had every right to engage in an artistic pastime on her own property! Who would dare say otherwise?

"Where would you like me?" she asked.

"How about in front of that fountain?" suggested Belldauer. "Maybe you could climb up onto the wall so I can capture those white flowers behind you."

"Honeysuckle," said Elsa. "During the nineteenth century," she added nervously, "teenaged girls were forbidden to sniff honeysuckle because the blossoms were believed to induce unseemly dreams."

"They're stunning flowers," he answered. "A perfect frame for a portrait of a stunning woman."

Elsa slid out of her slippers and inched along the stone wall as though advancing toward the end of a narrow branch. Belldauer stepped from behind the easel and watched as she allowed the robe to fall slowly from her shoulders.

How exposed she suddenly was! How vulnerable!

"I feel like a schoolgirl," said Elsa. "All jitters and nerves."

Belldauer stared at her body pensively, his fingertips pressed over his mouth. He looked as though he were discovering her for the first time. Elsa felt the shame building inside her. What a disappointment she must be! Here he was, clinging to a forty-five year old vision of youthful beauty, while all she had to offer were sagging breasts and cellulite. She wished she'd had the good sense to keep her clothes on.

Belldauer appeared troubled. More surprised than disappointed.

"That blue bracelet of yours," he said. "What was it? Cobalt?"

"I don't know," stammered Elsa.

"Do you still have it?'

"Maybe," she replied. "I could check for you."

Why had she said that? For the sake of the charade? Or because she was mortified to pose naked on a stone wall in front of a complete stranger? Morton Belldauer was, after all, nothing more than a stranger who'd written her a letter by mistake. Elsa reached for her robe. "I'll be right back," she said, and she scurried through the sliding glass doors into the living room.

Inside the house, of course, there was nothing Elsa could do except to wait until a sufficient interval of time had elapsed. She obviously did not own the other Elsa Kalamaransky's cobalt bracelet—or anything she might substitute in its place. If Belldauer learned the truth, she wondered, would he still track down the correct Elsa? Or would he cut his losses with her? Bruce, in Belldauer's shoes, would have worked his hardest to laugh off the entire episode. He certainly wouldn't have held her little falsehood against her. Quite the opposite: Bruce was one to appreciate a stunt so audacious and madcap. He might even have attempted something truly nutty, once he'd forgiven her—like inviting the other Elsa K. to join them both for dinner. But Elsa sensed a sober streak in Morton Belldauer that might prevent the man from looking beyond her deception so easily.

She waited for the grandfather clock to strike three. On the third peal, she strode back onto the veranda. Belldauer was seated on the edge of the stone wall, posed thoughtfully on the very stones where she was to model.

"I couldn't find the bracelet," said Elsa.

Belldauer nodded. His fingers kneaded his magnificent forehead.

"I couldn't find the bracelet," she continued, feeling her tongue grew loose in her mouth, "because I don't have the bracelet."

"How foolish of me to expect it," he answered. "It has been forty years…."

He was still scrutinizing her—probably trying to reconcile her naked body with the image frozen in his memory. Elsa drew in her breath.

"I *never* had the bracelet," she said. "I have a confession to make—"

Belldauer held up his hand. "Don't," he warned sharply.

"But I have to," continued Elsa. "I wish so much that I'd been that woman in your drawing class, but I wasn't."

"Please, don't," Belldauer repeated. Louder. "I already know."

"You know?"

She could tell by the deep sadness in his face that he'd seen through her.

"I believed you at first. Forty-five years *is* a very long time. But I knew the moment you removed your robe," said Belldauer. "You were so shy just now, so gloriously shy. How did you describe it? 'All nerves and jitters.' But the one thing I'll never forget about the woman who posed for us in Dr. Stanley's class was how confident she was, how comfortable in her own skin. I'd never seen such sophistication. That's not the sort of self-possession one ever forgets—not even after forty-five years."

So there it was. Over. Done. What a fool she had been.

"I'll assume this means you don't want me to pose for you," said Elsa.

Belldauer frowned at her, his face beset with gravity. This must have been the face he used when investigating mysteries in cuneiform. Elsa felt a dark, unforgiving ache pooling within her chest.

"Nothing survives forty-five years without evolving," he answered. "Not attraction, not love, not even memory. So maybe I'm imagining all that self-possession and sophistication." He stepped behind the easel decisively. "Of course, I still want you to pose," he said. "Just like you did in Dr. Stanley's class. Why should a lost cobalt bracelet make any difference?"

"What are you saying? That you want me to pretend I'm the right Elsa?"

"You are the right Elsa," he answered. "I'm sure of it."

So she climbed onto the fountain and let the robe slide once again from her shoulders. The breeze brushed gently against her bare skin, and she watched as Morton Belldauer copied her body, stroke by stroke, his hands moving with a powerful and coordinated intensity. Occasionally, their eyes met and she absorbed confidence from his certainty. She was already beginning to recall, with increasingly vivid detail, the much younger Morton Belldauer, surrounded by other intense young men, who had sketched her in Professor Stanley's figure drawing class so many years before.

Animal Control

Some small towns in New England still elect their dog catchers, but down here animal control has always been a civil service post. You log forty hours of coursework in chemical immobilization and euthanasia, pass a multiple choice exam, write out a check for eighty-five dollars payable to the Virginia Department of Agriculture—and before you can say sweet Jesus on a flapjack, you've got a job you can't lose, short of sticking your pecker in a rabid groundhog. But that doesn't mean it's all country ham and gravy. Not hardly. You don't know stress until you've told the parents of a nine year old kid that you're going to put down his beloved Lassie or Old Yeller. Which is why, when the field supervisor pokes his head into the dayroom, I get a wallop of those cat-on-a-hot-roof jitters. There's just me and Josie today—Lisa May's out on her honeymoon in Las Vegas—so I know some unlucky critter somewhere has my number.

It's nearly noon and I'm reading a book about hoaxes. My sister-in-law's recommendation. Josie is cooking up catfish in a pan. The dayroom smells like frying.

"Ready to earn your bread, Mr. Dipple?" asks the field manager. He's not a bad egg, as bosses go, but he's third-generation veterinarian, so he thinks he's just a speck better than everybody else. He insists on calling us Mr. Dipple, and Miss Jackson, and Miss Bickmore—though I guess Miss Bickmore's going to be Mrs. Butts from now on—and we're supposed to call him Dr. Molinary, at least to his face. As if we work in a grammar school or a post office. What takes the cake about Doc Molinary is he wears cream-colored suits, like Errol Flynn, even in winter. "I have police already on the scene," he says. "County patrol on their way."

"Let me guess. Another stolen monkey." We've got a big research hospital in Spotsylvania County now—and last year a gang of animal liberation folks attempted to spring free a chimpanzee. Damn monkey went bonkers. We spent nearly six hours trying to coax it down from the ferris wheel at the fairgrounds. "If I buy another thousand bananas at that Winn Dixie, the manager will have me committed."

"No monkey business, I'm afraid," says Molinary. "Try a tiger."

I look at my watch. April 1st is still two days away. "A tiger?"

"On the loose in Hollow Grove. Escaped from an outfit licensed in North Carolina. The Forepaugh Family Traveling Circus." He hands me the manila folder that contains the intake sheet. "You'd better hurry. It's seems our tiger has already made away with an eight month old baby."

Josie flips off the gas range. "So much for lunch," she says.

"Good luck, Mr. Dipple. Good luck, Miss Jackson," says the field manager, a bit too formal—like some Old West mayor sending John Wayne to fight bandits. "You go after the tiger. I'll handle the reporters. We'll see who comes back alive."

Doc Molinary smiles, pleased with his own joke. I smile back. I don't bother to tell him that his fly is unzipped.

~

It's a gorgeous day, probably over seventy. Makes you think those Global Warming people know what they're talking about. The birch trees along Princess Anne Street have started to leaf. Robins are feeding in front of the Washington Mutual. Young mothers crowd the walkways beside the Rappahannock. It's hard to remember that, a century before I was born, General Burnside lost twelve thousand men trying to take this ground from Lee's Virginians. Don't get me wrong: I'm not some wacko with a Confederate battle flag on his bumper. I've got nothing personal against people moving out here from Washington or Alexandria. Everybody has to live somewhere. I just think it's important a guy know what happened in a place before he showed up.

I adjust the rearview mirror and ease the van into traffic. It feels odd to be driving with the sirens. "There used to be these giant elm trees all along here," I say to Josie.

"I'm sure there were. Good, sturdy lynching trees," says Josie. She's only in her late-twenties, but she's the first Black animal control officer in Virginia. Her fiancé teaches criminal justice at Mary Washington. "Say, you're the movie buff. Isn't there an old movie about a tiger on the loose? Something with Gregory Peck?"

It's true. I do watch a lot of movies. My marriage to Gwen is like that.

118

"*Bringing up Baby*," I say. "Katherine Hepburn keeps it for a pet. But it's Cary Grant, not Gregory Peck. And it's a leopard, not a tiger."

"Well, pardon me for living," says Josie, grinning.

"On the subject of tigers, you got a location in Hollow Grove?"

Josie reads me an address from the folder. She must sense something in my reaction, because she asks, "You familiar with the place?"

I know the Minard place, all right. I grew up out in Hollow Grove—back when it was the only subdivision between D.C. and Richmond. All that land had once been Minard land. Years later, when I was at Virginia State, I took a class in Southern history, and the professor, who had this thing against suburbs, kept calling Hollow Grove "Levittown for crackers." That's total bullshit, of course. My papa taught accounting at a private high school and my mama did social work for the county. But there's no point explaining things to people who don't want to know them.

"I used to be familiar with the place. Before you were born," I tell Josie. "Screwy family lived out there, but I'm sure they're all gone now." I take the Hollow Grove exit off the turnpike and cross the railroad tracks onto Culpepper Avenue. "Fact is, I'm surprised the old place is still standing."

Or maybe it's not still standing, I realize. The same address doesn't have to mean the same building. It could be a Chevy dealership these days. Or a porno theater. That's why I never drive out here. If I had kids, maybe I'd want to show off my old stomping grounds. Who knows? But I don't have kids.

It turns out the entire subdivision is gone. Ploughed over by the new Interstate to Charlottesville. There's a motel where my house stood. It's got a Dutch theme. Windmill over the office. Tulips and daffodils out front. That's one thing we never have a shortage of in this lifetime. Bad ideas. I don't tell Josie I used to live here.

Then we turn up Lady Randolph Street—and it's the same house. An old colonial with two chimneys. There's about six gazillion squad cars out front—state police, Spotsylvania County, Prince George County, Fredericksburg traffic enforcement—not to mention enough fire trucks for an Independence Day parade. The television crews have set up shop on the other side of a sawhorse cordon. I'm not even out of the van when the commander on-scene, this huge bald guy with a walrus mustache, is practically up my nose. "You animal control?" he demands.

"That's what it says on the van," I say.

"It's about time," he says. "This one takes the cake. I got an escaped tiger snatching a baby off the back porch and carrying it up a beech tree."

"It is injured?"

"Hard to say. You can't see much with all those the evergreens. It was crying for a while, for what it's worth, but now it's stopped."

I shake my head. "Not the kid. The tiger."

"Oh, the tiger," says the commander. "How the hell should I know?"

"Well, let's go have a look," I say.

Josie hands me the tranquilizer gun and we start up the steep driveway. That's when I see her. She's much thinner today, you could even say too thin, but she still carries herself like a fat girl. Her hair is gray as steel wool. It matches her sweater. You can tell she's been crying, but now she's got this totally blank look and she's rocking back and forth like some sort of Bible-thumper. Her husband isn't half bad looking. A few years younger than she is, not too short—only his face is a bit blotchy. He's got his arm around Evangelina's shoulder.

I steel myself and walk directly up to her.

"Good morning, Miss Minard," I say.

She looks puzzled. "Mrs. Stevens, now," she says. "Do I know you?"

Not a hint of recognition. But I guess she has other things on her mind.

"Animal control," is what I answer. "Tell me what happened."

~

This might be a good point to mention that I wasn't a popular teenager. I didn't cut it as an athlete, I certainly was no rocket scientist in the classroom, and it didn't help any to be the son of Melvin Dipple, who taught bookkeeping with a pencil over his ear and chalk-prints on the seat of his trousers. My brother compensated for his shortcomings with humor—and he won permanent social acceptance after he filled the deputy headmaster's Oldsmobile Tornado with six thousand nickel-plated ball bearings. I tried to follow in Albert's footsteps, but I just wasn't funny. By eleventh grade, I threw in the towel on cool. Instead, I took up birdwatching.

While Carter and Reagan bickered over leading the Free World, I went thrashing through the underbrush for woodpeckers and wrens. I wore a mesh pith helmet that my brother bought for a summer-stock production of *Lawrence of Arabia*. The hat came with a leather chin strap and a veil of mosquito netting. I also had a pair of Zeiss field glasses my Grandpa Cavanaugh brought back from North Africa. He was an artillery officer during the war. Probably the only Dipple or Cavanaugh ever to do anything important. For camouflage, I spread guacamole on my cheeks.

My goal was to spot all eight hundred species in the Peterson guide. Not that I cared so much about birds. What I wanted was accomplishment. Fossils or model horses would have done as well. But having picked birds, I hunted them with a vengeance.

Mostly, I kept to the subdivision. Sometimes I crossed the high meadow and ducked under the split-rail fence into the Minard's enormous backyard. The overgrown tea roses were great for hummingbirds, except when the hounds were outside. And the Minard's property was like a hidden amusement park. Some of the money from the farmland had gone into a private playground. A swingset. Monkey bars. A heart-shaped sandbox. They also had clay tennis courts, but they didn't maintain them. Being in the Minard yard never felt like trespassing, but I didn't dare ride on the swings. And then one evening—a long twilight in early spring—I was watching two large black birds perched atop the Minard's weathervane when Mr. Minard snuck up behind me.

Mr. Minard was tall and slender with a baby face, but in his forties he already walked with a stoop, and his skin was the color of cucumber pulp. I knew all about the man without ever having met him. If you lived in Hollow Grove, this was what you talked about. Darwin Minard had been raised by his mama—up north—then came back to the homestead with an overweight wife and the ugliest baby anybody could remember. The wife had sung opera once, but had a tumor on her voice box.

Mr. Minard dabbed his forehead with his handkerchief—as though encountering me was a cause of considerable exertion. "See anything interesting?" he asked.

"Ravens," I said defensively.

"Hmmm. Look like crows to me."

Mr. Minard broke off a sprig of forsythia and sniffed it approvingly. "How do you know they're not crows?" he asked.

They were crows, of course. We both knew that. But I also realized he thought I was a peeping Tom, which I wasn't.

"They're too large for crows," I said. "Their beaks are too thick."

He nodded. "Ravens. How do you like that?"

Mr. Minard snapped off several more sprays of forsythia and tucked them into a wet dish towel. He was assembling a bouquet.

"You think she's pretty, don't you?" he asked.

"Who's pretty?"

But just then I caught sight of Evangelina Minard standing at one of the dormer windows under the weathervane. She was the year behind me in school. Walleyed. Fat as a Turk. In the habit of fanning her neck with her hands. There was a limerick about Evangelina and a suckling pig graffitied in one of the boys' bathrooms.

Mr. Minard reached into his pants pocket and toyed with his keys.

"What's your name?" he asked.

I considered a secret identity. All I could think of were Clark Kent and Peter Parker. "Jethro Dipple," I said.

"Well, Jethro Dipple," he said, "When I was your age, I used to hide in the *au pair's* closet. Fjola from Iceland. *Fj-o-la.* She was probably about twenty-five years old—and she would strip down in front of the mirror to look at herself. One day, I sneezed and she caught me—and I was positive she was going to tell my mother, but she didn't. For the rest of that summer, she let me sit on the bed while I watched."

"I should go home now," I said.

"No need for that," he said. "You're missing the whole point of my story."

"I wasn't doing anything," I said.

"I tell you what," said Mr. Minard. "Why don't you stay for supper? I'm sure Evangelina would be delighted."

I tried to object. Being un-cool was one thing. Being known as the guy who spied on Evangelina Minard was another. But what could I do? You don't have leverage when you're sixteen and covered in avocado dip. Either I followed Evangeline's father up to the big house, or I made a chancy dash through the brush. I searched for a break in the azalea hedge—but deep down I was a coward. Soon enough, I found myself standing in the Minard's big country kitchen.

The room's walls were large square timbers. All except around the hearth, which was exposed yellow brick. Assorted pots hung from the rafters. Silver candlesticks sat on the walnut dinner table. But there was also a modern oven, a dishwasher, and a double-doored Kelvinator refrigerator. The oven stood open, and a servant girl with an enormous rump was bent over it, rotating a turkey. Mrs. Minard hovered nearby, sipping a vermillion cocktail. She was big, but with shorts legs. Like a cartoon ox. Not un-pretty, just fat. Mr. Minard said I'd come to have dinner with Evangeline.

"Does he have a name?" asked Mrs. Minard, her voice like sandpaper.

They both looked at me. "Jethro Dipple," I said.

"Dipple. I know Dipple," she said. "He's the one with the tiny little balls."

She meant the ball bearings. "That's my brother," I said.

"It seems like we're being inundated by Dipples," said Mrs. Minard—and she laughed fiercely. "No matter. I think it's about time Evangelina had a boyfriend."

As though on cue, the daughter walked into the kitchen. She was chewing gum.

"There you are, darling," said Mrs. Minard. "I was telling your friend here that you could use a boyfriend."

This was the only time—for a split second—that I felt bad for Evangelina Minard. Because we were not friends. We'd never exchanged two words in our lives. And we weren't going to be friends. Or I felt bad because the idea of her having a boyfriend—ever—seemed so totally impossible. The poor girl gasped when she saw me. She looked as though she'd just dropped a baby. "Oh my God," she said.

"Jethro here has been attempting to spy on you," said Mr. Minard.

I hid the field glasses behind my folded arms. Shame burned the tips of my ears.

"Gross," exclaimed Evangelina.

"You should be flattered," said Mr. Minard. "I told you it was only a matter of time before you turned into a swan."

This made Evangelina blush. "Daddy!"

"I have an idea," said Mrs. Minard. "Darling, we still have some time before supper is ready. Why don't you model for your friend here?" The woman turned to me and added: "Evangelina is going to be a great stage actress someday. She's very talented. All she needs to do is reduce a bit."

"Please, Mommy," said Evangelina. "I don't want to."

"It will be fun," said Mrs. Minard. "And good experience. Especially with company."

I looked to the servant for help, but the girl was painting butter on the turkey as though nothing were out of the ordinary. If Evangelina's father had turned me in for peeping, I could have lived with that. Somehow. But going from peeper to "company" was downright freaky. Evangelina must have thought so too. Her small dark eyes had taken on a watery, desperate look.

"Let's ask the boy," said her mother. "Jethro, wouldn't you like Evangelina to model for you?"

It crossed my mind that she might mean naked modeling. Or at least lingerie. In that house, anything was possible. "I guess so," I said. When I was sixteen, even Evangelina Minard was worth seeing in the nude.

My imagination quickly got the better of me. I was dreaming of bikinis, silk garters, kimonos from Japan. Evangelina Minard casually stepping out of peignoirs in front of floor-to-ceiling mirrors. But my fantasies quickly came down crashing. The daughter disappeared through the kitchen door and returned an eternity later wearing a smock-like maroon evening gown a good forty years out of style. She had a string of black pearls around her neck and a hideous costume brooch pinned to her chest. The brooch was jade green and shaped like a moth. Evangeline posed with her plump hand on her equally plump hip. She had trouble balancing herself on her five-inch heels. Meanwhile, I tried to wipe off the guacamole with my sleeve.

"My grand-aunt left us a whole steamer trunk of winter dresses," said Mrs. Minard. That explained the sudden, pungent odor of naphthalene. "My grand-aunt was a Delacroix from Savannah."

"Isn't she stunning?" asked Mr. Minard. "Who do you think she looks more like—Marlene Dietrich or Greta Garbo?"

"You're showing your age, dearest," answered his wife. "I'm sure he's never heard of either of them. Try Farrah Fawcett or Raquel Welch."

It struck me that both of the adult Minards might be drunk. Mrs. Minard did indeed pour herself another cocktail. "Why don't you show us something décolleté, darling?" she urged her daughter "Maybe the lilac chiffon?" And Evangelina dutifully tottered out of the room.

"I tell you, Jethro Dipple, some young man out there is going to be very lucky one of these days," said Mr. Minard. "He's going to win the heart of a spectacular girl." I instantly thought of winning a piñata at the Mexican raffle. "And I don't mind saying, he's also going to find himself in an extremely advantageous position financially."

That's when I realized he knew the truth. They both knew. That their daughter was hideous as sin. Somehow, that made the fashion show even less bearable. I nearly bowled over the servant girl on my race toward the rear steps.

I can't imagine Evangelina's reaction when she showed up in her lilac chiffon evening gown—and her audience was gone. But she couldn't have been none too happy. By the following afternoon, the entire school knew I'd been spying on her.

~

So here I am. Face to face with the girl who ruined me in high school. And also the lucky guy who finally won the piñata. In the same overgrown yard where I was once afraid to climb on the monkey bars. But everything's totally different now, of course. Because twenty-five years have gone by, and they've got a baby up a tree, and I'm packing the only tranquilizer gun in miles. Fate can have a mean sense of humor.

I wait patiently while Evangelina tells me about the tiger. "I was inside hardly half a minute," she says. "Just taking Daddy's breakfast up to his room. I saw it through the upstairs window."

"You live with your father, Mrs. Stevens?" I ask.

Evangelina nods. She is sobbing again. Her husband adds: "She takes care of him. He's not right anymore, you understand."

So the old man's gone off the deep end. I can't help taking some pleasure in this.

"Do you think there's a chance....?" Mr. Stevens lets his sentence trail away.

"We'll do our best," I say. "We always do." I'm not sure why I add this second part—maybe I don't want him to think we're cooking up anything special.

I turn away abruptly and follow the commander out to the tree. Josie is on her cell phone, discussing big cats with the Capital Zoo. We've also been joined by a ruddy, muscular guy in his seventies, a real Jacques Lalanne type, who keeps the animals for the Forepaugh family. His name is Ted Serspinski. His wardrobe staples are panama hat, alligator boots and bola tie. "The darnedest thing," he says, not too fazed. "But I suppose that's what we have insurance for." He has mentioned the welfare of the tiger, Duchess, half a dozen times. He hasn't said a word about the baby.

We stop under the tree. It's in a thicket of cedars, so you can't see very far up. Occasionally, there's a flurry of branches. "You're wrong," I tell the commander. "It's not a beech tree. It's a basswood."

"You fucking kidding?" asks the commander. "You a fucking botanist or something?"

I stay deadpan. "I wouldn't kid you. It's definitely a basswood."

The commander doesn't know what to make of this. He's resting one hand on the handle of his Billy club and the other on his service revolver. But I guess he thinks I'm a whackjob—and there's no sense arguing with a whackjob. "If it's a basswood, it's a basswood," he says. "You think you can shoot the damn thing from down here?"

I balance the tranquilizer gun on my shoulder and aim into the greenery. "Not a chance in hell," I say. "Maybe I can get a better angle from the roof of the house."

The circus guy doesn't like this idea. "You can't be serious," he objects. "She could fall out of the tree."

"Goddammit," says the commander. "If you get a shot, shoot."

"Are you sure about that?" I ask. "He might have a point. What if it knocks the kid out of the tree on the way down?"

The commander looks at me like I killed his dog. "Goddamit," he says again.

I turn to Josie. "Any ideas?"

"Actually, I do," she says. "According to Washington, we shouldn't do anything. If it hasn't harmed the kid yet, it's not going to. We should just sit on our hands until it decides it's ready to come down."

The commander spits into the dust. "So we're just supposed to wait for it to make the first move?"

"That looks like the plan," I say.

"They're going to send out their cat-keeper, but it may take a while," says Josie. "He's on jury duty and they've got to track him down."

That just takes the cake. Jury duty. Another lucky break for the Minards.

I send Josie back to the truck for my camping chair. Then I cozy up with my sister-in-law's book: DUPED: The 100 Greatest Deceptions of

All Time. But it's hard to focus. I keep thinking about Evangelina, and about meeting her like this, and about how everything turned out. She's obviously not a great stage actress. And I'm not some expert on big cats who gets called in from D.C. I'm not even a vet or a cop. I'm just some civil service lackey with a dietician wife and no kids who knows a helluva lot about black and white movies. All in all, we're both rather damn ordinary. Which is pretty okay, I suppose, once you get used to it. But sometimes you can't help wondering how things might be different: If I'd been popular in high school. If I'd married Evangelina Minard. If Gwen hadn't had a hysterectomy. I fold the hoax book on my chest and lean back for a one-eyed nap.

At some point, a uniformed cop shows up with a bag of sandwiches. Somebody must have gotten his orders crossed, because another cop appears ten seconds later with two pizzas and a case of Dr. Pepper. It feels kind of strange to be chowing down while there's an escaped tiger in the tree above you—but that's what public service is like. You do what you can do. And sometimes you do what you can't do. In between, you stop for a pastrami on rye bread.

"You want to hear something amazing?" I ask the circus guy.

"What's that?"

"In England back in the '50s, they showed a television special on the spaghetti harvest in Italy. It was part of an April Fool's Day hoax. And people bought it—hook, line and sinker."

"Is that so?"

"They got letters from people asking where they could buy spaghetti trees."

I can tell the guy doesn't give two slaps about hoaxes. Probably has no idea he's standing half a mile from Stonewall Jackson's HQ. Or that in my twelfth grade, Duke Crenshaw passed around a petition to change the Virginia state bird to the "Peeping Dipple." Why should he want to know about me? All the circus guy cares about is his cats. And all Evangelina cares about is her baby. And all Doc Molinary cares about is keeping his first name out of the public record. We're a bunch of screw-ups, aren't we? People, I mean.

"You want another sandwich?" I ask circus guy. "We've got bologna, corned beef…and this one looks like bologna and turkey."

That's when the commotion erupts behind us. It's Evangelina's husband. The cops are trying to restrain him, but he won't back off.

"Let the guy through," I say.

The commander glares at me. "Let him through," he says.

Stevens comes directly to me. He must think I'm in charge. The guy must have come straight from the office—he's still wearing his tie and a tweed jacket with elbow pads. The tie has these tiny white anchors on it.

"What's up?" I ask.

"We've been waiting and waiting and waiting. This is killing us," he says, short of breath. "Can't you do something already."

The circus guy is standing next to me. "We've got to wait her down. It's the safest for both of them."

Stevens goes up like someone's lit a firecracker in his ass. "Both of them!" he shouts. "That's my goddamn son in that tree. If you don't do something—right goddamn now—I'm swear I'm going to do something myself."

The commander warns him to calm down. Like that does any good. Nothing to relax a panicked dad like a cop flexing muscle.

"You want us to do something," I say. "Okay, we'll do something."

"What about waiting?" demands circus guy.

"You heard the man. He wants action," I answer. "Anyone know how to get one of those machines they use on utility poles? You know what I mean....Apple pickers?"

"Cherry pickers," says Josie.

"That's right," I say. "Get me one of those. Fast."

~

I've never ridden in one of these things before. For ordinary house pets, we go up in a ladder. Not glamorous, but it does the job. And it's cheap. Cherry pickers, on the other hand, are a once-in-a-lifetime opportunity, so I'm set on making the most of this.

At first, the guy down below does all of the steering. He pulls his levers and I'm up at the first branches, then higher than the Minard's roof. But it's me who has to direct the final few yards. "Left," I call out. "Up. Left. More left." The basket of the cherry picker snaps cedar branches as it moves. "Stop," I command. "Right there."

"Can you see it?" Josie shouts.

I can see it, all right. The tiger's just lying there, on a thick basswood limb. Minding its own damn business. And the baby's just lying there too. In a fork between branches. Eyes closed. Scratch marks on its bare chest—but tree scratches, not claw marks. The child is quiet as a gravestone, but he's still breathing. I raise the tranquilizer gun to my shoulder. At first, I take aim at the tiger. But then it strikes me that I could just as easily hit the baby. Get back at Evangelina for twelfth grade. Take a little bit of the random power in the world for myself. Mistakes do happen. Otherwise, I've got a clean record. Who'd ever know the difference?

I focus on the baby, then the cat, then the baby. Beyond them, though a break in the cedars, I can see all of Fredericksburg: the glistening Rappahannock coiling its way toward the horizon, the bell tower of Mary Washington's, the churches and tobacco warehouses and the strip malls spreading south toward Richmond. My wife's out there too, probably watching this on the TV in the nurse's station. Below me, Josie and the circus guy and Evangelina's husband are all shading their eyes against the sun. I guess this is what it means to have your life flash before your eyes.

"You all right up there?" calls Josie.

"I'm fine," I shout back. "Give me a second."

And then I fire. Straight into the cat's shank. The animal jolts upright—and then crumples, crashing through the thicket below.

I hear screaming at ground level. The circus guy cursing. The commander ordering people to back off. Evangelina wailing, "My baby! My baby!" I pull the cherry picker toward the branch and scoop up the kid in my arms.

I'm still not sure I made the right call. Truth is, I'm still not sure a baby's worth more alive than a tiger. But it's not my job to figure that out. No point in asking questions about what's fair and what's right. No point at all. Because the danger is you'll start answering them. And that's great if you're the President or something, but not so good if you're an ordinary guy. I know where I'll end up if I start asking questions like that, and answering them, and it's no place I ever want to be.

The Author

Jacob M. Appel's most recent works include a novel, *The Biology of Luck,* and an essay collection, *Phoning Home.* The stories in *The Magic Laundry* stem from his work as a psychiatrist in New York City, and his particular interest in how ordinary people cope with extraordinary challenges. He hopes these stories will encourage his readers to place themselves in the shoes of his protagonists and to ask themselves how they would handle the tribulations confronted by his characters. What would you do if your daughter returned home from college with a stolen baboon? Or if you operated a Laundromat and the washing machines gained a reputation for performing minor miracles? In the course of practicing medicine, Dr. Appel has observed that the most extraordinary things do happen to ordinary people. Every day, in every city and town, often drawing little public notice. Yet few events are more extraordinary that the publication of a book—especially a collection of short stories—and as a strikingly ordinary person himself, Dr. Appel looks forward to both his own reaction and yours.

The Magic Laundry
by Jacob M. Appel
Winner of the 2014 Serena McDonald Kennedy Fiction Award

Previous Winners

Dwight Yates	*Haywire Hearts and Slide Trombones*	2006
Brian Bedard	*Grieving on the Run*	2007
Kathy Flann	*Smoky Ordinary*	2008
Wendy Marcus	*Polyglot*	2009
Starkey Flythe	*Driving With Hand Controls*	2010
Richard Fellinger	*They Hover Over Us*	2011
Dwight Holing	*California Works*	2012
John Zeugner	*Under Hiroshima, Collected Stories*	2013

Serena McDonald Kennedy

Serena McDonald Kennedy was born in 1850 on the fourth of July. She was the fifth of seven daughters and the ninth of 12 children, of James and Serena Swain McDonald in Thomas County, Georgia. She was descended from Alexander McDonald, a Scottish Highlander, who fought with General James Oglethorpe at the Battle of Bloody Marsh, which saved Florida from the Spanish. His son was our Revolutionary hero.

Her father and mother, after marriage, settled on a farm between the McDonald and Swain plantations, later occupying the Reese plantation and finally the Swain plantation where they lived until their deaths. A town grew up around their home site named McDonald, Georgia, now known as Pavo, making James one of the first real estate developers of the area.

Serena, although far down the list of girls, had her mother's name, one, it was said, that fit her personality. Only a few years after her birth, her father would go to war as a Lieutenant-Colonel in the Confederacy, and she would lose a brother in the War Between the States. We have in our possession a long letter written in beautiful Spencerian script from her brother, Kenneth, a Captain, on April 20, 1863 (when she was 13 and he was 23), from "near Fredricksburg, Virginia." He wrote of the beauty* of Spring in Virginia, and as a postscript, he said: "You will excuse this miserable bad written thing of a letter; for God's sake don't show it." Only two weeks later, he was wounded at Chancellorsville and died three weeks later.

Serena was 30 years old before McDonald, Georgia, became Pavo, because of a conflict with the larger town named McDonough. At that time, a Mr. Peacock was Postmaster, and wanted the town to have his name, so in forwarding a group of names for selection to

At 35, Serena was what was then generally called "an old maid," who came to the community of Enon in Thomas County as a school teacher. There she met and married John Thomas Kennedy, ten years her junior. Tom, as he was called, had lost a young wife and child in childbirth, and he and Serena began a life together that lasted for 40 years, until Serena died at the age of 75. Tom died 10 years later. They were the parents of four children, the second of whom was my father, Archibald Randolph Kennedy.

My grandmother was a great believer in education, and to our ultimate benefit, she saw that my father went to prep school and college, unusual in the rural area in which our family lived. His education influenced our family in many ways, and I attribute my love of literature to that heritage.

Although Serena died before I was born, my mother, Adeline Kennedy, was so devoted to her mother-in-law that she quoted her often and patterned our development after what she learned from her mother-in-law. My sister, Martha Stephenson, my brother, William Kennedy, and I are her only grandchildren living today. It is a great honor for us to have the Serena McDonald Kennedy Award named for her.

Barbara Kennedy Passmore

*"The weather has turned warm and pleasant at last. The cold icy blast of winter has past and all nature looks revived. The sufferings of a cold hard winter seem to have been all forgotten and a few warm days have induced the trees to put forth their Buds and Blossoms. Everything seems to be in a high state of pleasure and glee.
Everything is beautiful and harmonious.
It's a bright Sabbath morning..."*
–Kenneth McDonald